W9-BTS-166

Miss Ryder's Memoirs

Laura Matthews

A SIGNET BOOK

NEW AMERICAN LIBRARY

For Kay and Miranda, with thanks for their help
and encouragement

NAL BOOKS ARE AVAILABLE AT QUANTITY DISCOUNTS WHEN USED TO
PROMOTE PRODUCTS OR SERVICES. FOR INFORMATION PLEASE WRITE TO
PREMIUM MARKETING DIVISION, NAL PENGUIN INC., 1633 BROADWAY,
NEW YORK, NEW YORK 10019

SIGNET, SIGNET CLASSIC, MENTOR, ONYX, PLUME,
MERIDIAN and NAL BOOKS are published by NAL PENGUIN INC.,
1633 Broadway, New York, New York 10019

First Printing, September, 1988

1 2 3 4 5 6 7 8 9

PRINTED IN THE UNITED STATES OF AMERICA

·1·

Several strange things happened that summer. *He* says it would be a great mistake to write an account of that time, for some prying eye might chance upon it, but I must confess my fingers itch to write it down. In time we are bound to forget the details and it may seem as though nothing out of the ordinary happened. But I know better now. So, against *his* advice, which I am not always governed by, I shall spell out my adventures in glorious detail—and hide the manuscript somewhere truly safe. Perhaps a hundred years from now, when our bones molder in the village cemetery, someone will come upon my account and it will shock them. So much the better.

The first thing I have to say is that I was raised quite properly by conscientious and loving parents. They should not be held responsible for any unbecoming behavior of mine; after all, my sister, Amanda, has never once done anything out of the ordinary. What a dull life she has led! But that is neither here nor there. My brother, Robert, on the other hand, has been a little wild, but people seem to expect that. Boys are always granted more indulgence than girls, if you wish my opinion. *He* says my opinion on such subjects is not worth a tinker's dam, but he's biased, being a male himself.

It's true that I was raised to be a lady of quality, and

even *he* can't deny that in most respects I fulfill the role remarkably well. Actually, what *he* would say is that I look the part because I'm small and have fine features, which give the illusion of a demureness that I do not in the least possess. Never mind. For the most part, people believe what they see: Catherine Ryder wears her auburn hair in a decorous style and keeps her lovely green eyes lowered in a most becoming modesty.

He laughs at my saying that, of course. If people wish to see me as modest, who am I to disillusion them? My eyes are a dead giveaway to my sentiments and it's only reasonable that I should keep them prudently lowered on certain occasions. I was born with a sense of the absurd that very few people share. But to get on with my story.

It was a mild summer, with fairly regular bouts of rain. By the time July came, I was grateful for a few inordinately hot days. Amanda sits in the shrubbery and fans herself when it's hot. I go to the pond. Ever since we were very young children, Robert and I had gone to the pond. It meant escaping from our nanny, but we were perfectly capable of that. Of course, a time came when Robert himself became "modest" and would no longer go to the pond with me, but by then I had quite learned what a youthful male body looked like.

The first, and only, time we tried to take Amanda with us, she very nearly put a permanent period to our escapades. I had to bribe her with a whole summer's worth of sugarplums to keep her from confessing our destination and activity. For Papa had taught Robert to swim, and Robert taught me. We would have taught Amanda, but when she saw that Robert meant to take off his clothes, she ran screaming from the glade. Just like a silly child. Really, it's a wonder I speak to her! She hasn't changed much in the last dozen years.

That summer Robert was still in London when the great heat descended on Cambridgeshire, so I knew I should not be discovered if I took a dip in the pond. He would have been surprised to see how his skinny sister had filled out in some places, because he still tended to think of me as a child. That's another thing men do: they grow up and become men, but they think females remain girls forever and ever.

Still, I have to admit that it was Robert who discovered our perfect swimming hole. No one else seems to have found it because there's a decoy: a large, obvious pond, a charming part of the landscape, with its placid oval of green, clear water. No one would dare to swim in that open situation, where all the world, riding past on the road to Newmarket, might catch a glimpse of one. But along the northern edge of the water there's a stand of trees beyond a jumble of boulders. The boulders are not inviting, with their sharp edges and crumbling surfaces. And even if someone were to explore them, they would hardly notice the one narrow passage through them where the water meanders past into a special pocket of the glade.

Rather shallow, the lagoon itself is protected by more boulders, with the stand of trees only coming close at one point. It's so secluded that I've never felt the least fear of detection there. So off I set on the first Tuesday in July, when it was so hot that even Amanda's even temper was somewhat frayed, refusing rather abruptly when I invited her to walk with me.

"Walk? In this heat? My dear Catherine, you must be teasing," she said as she plied her fan faster. "Mama would not approve of a walk in this heat."

"I'm persuaded she would allow me my eccentricity," I retorted. Mama has a few eccentricities of her own.

I wore my old jonquil muslin because I knew it was one of the few garments that I could don again with reasonable ease. These high-waisted dresses do have their advantages, say what you will. I also wore a wide-brimmed bonnet to protect my face from the sun. Not that I'm missish about a slight coloring from the glare, but it has a tendency to bring out my freckles, and that Mama would disapprove of excessively. I have to admit that even I have some doubts about the attractiveness of freckles. On the face, at any rate.

Amanda frowned at me as I strolled by her, heading for the pond. "You really ought to carry your parasol, Catherine."

Naturally I didn't pay the least heed to her. Whether I listen or not, it gives her consequence to offer me advice, I think. Being so well informed on what is proper, and sharing the information, makes her feel more grown up. She's only eighteen, and she resents the fact that I'm two years older and don't pay the least attention to all her absurd standards of behavior. Goodness, I shouldn't want to grow dull as Amanda. *He* says there's no chance of such a thing happening.

The sun beat down on the narrow path I followed, making the dirt spring out in little puffs with each footfall. I could hardly wait to dispose of my gown and shift; they never feel so constricting as in the heat. In my walk I passed no one, though there were various animals that my dog sported after. Dutch, the dog, is fond of galloping after rabbits and squirrels, but he's never caught one, thank heaven. Even Dutch seemed a bit dragged down by the weather. I very clearly saw one rabbit that he made no move to follow. His big basset ears drooped almost to the ground.

Before passing through the narrow opening to the hidden lagoon, I casually surveyed the area around me, looking for anyone in the summer-droning landscape. The pond was well out of sight of our manor house, and mostly surrounded by grazing land. In this kind of weather there were cows standing belly-deep in the cool water. The road beyond would have an occasional horse and rider, or a carriage, but there was nothing visible on the nearest stretch at the moment. I quickly slipped through the passage in the rocks.

This isn't as easy as it sounds, because even when you've taken your shoes off, the stone under the water is both slippery and sharp. There are several places where one can get a good handhold, but where you can't, it's difficult to make your way without falling, especially when you have shoes and stockings in your hands. Dutch makes a great production of following, splashing about in the water as though it were required of him. It's a wonder I wasn't drenched by the time I reach the second, smaller pond.

Only one boulder here is flat enough to lie on to dry off, so it's where I leave my clothes. The jonquil muslin looked like a splash of bright paint on the weathered rock. Beside it I placed my rolled shift, my shoes, my stockings, and my bonnet. There was almost no breeze, so I didn't have to worry about my clothes blowing into the water.

Having had only a moderate amount of experience, and only a meager amount of instruction, my swimming is not perhaps as dexterous as it might be. The important thing is that I can keep myself afloat and paddle my way across the narrow stretch of water. There is something deliciously exciting about one's naked body gliding through the water. If you haven't tried it, you would never credit the pleasure of the water's caress.

I'm not a stranger to my body, as Amanda is. I doubt if she's ever looked at herself in a mirror when she had no clothes on. Why, she's embarrassed if you find her in her nightgown without a dressing gown over it. She calls this behavior "modesty." And wears her gowns so long no view of her ankle is possible to inflame some male who happened to glance down. In my experience that is almost never the direction a man's gaze takes, but Amanda merely waves aside such considerations.

Because I ride and walk and swim and take part in any kind of sport that I am not absolutely forbidden, my body is rather firm and compact. Amanda's is rounder, which some people seem to think is just how a woman's body should be, but I'm not the least envious of her. To maintain so pale and soft an image one apparently has to sit in the shade all day and lounge on a sofa—not straining one's eyes—all evening. That sort of life is not for me! I should die of boredom.

But to continue.

The tiny lagoon wasn't as warm that day as it had been many others. I had to swim briskly to dissipate the chill, but after a few minutes my body adjusted. I was floating on my back, with my eyes closed, when I heard a very distinct male voice ask, "Is this some new activity in the country? Really, I should have left London long since if I'd known."

Occasionally I am quick-witted. This was not one of those occasions. The only thing I could think to do was drop down under the water. This had the disadvantage of being a position in which I could not breathe. I was forced to surface again, knowing full well that the water was clear as glass. "Go away," I shouted, afraid to even look toward the rocks from whence his voice issued. It was not a boy's voice. This was a full-grown man, and one I'd never met, from the sound of that deep, amused voice. Believe me, I'd have recognized any of the locals and given them a piece of my mind.

"I can't very well go away when I see a maiden in distress," he insisted. "Why, I believe a young woman has fallen into the pond and may be in need of my assistance."

"I don't need your help. I can swim perfectly well."

"I wouldn't precisely agree with you on that. You do more of a dog paddle than a stroke, but I suppose we mustn't be splitting hairs. Shall I join you?"

"No!" The very suggestion forced my eyes to find him. He was perched above the spot where my jonquil muslin lay. Not far enough away for the view of my body to be denied him. "It's quite ungentlemanlike of you to sit there gaping at me. A fellow with even a modicum of manners would have long since disappeared."

"A fellow with no spirit of adventure perhaps. Why, it's not every day a fellow happens on a beautiful mermaid splashing about in a pond under his nose. I really am tempted to join you," he said, putting a hand up to loosen his starched neckcloth.

"Don't you dare!" It was at that moment that I remembered Dutch and had my famous idea. "I shall set my dog on you if you make any such attempt."

"You mean this wild beast?" He shifted to reveal that he was petting Dutch where the dog crouched slavishly near his feet.

"No, not that one," I snapped. "There's another one and he'll rip your throat out."

"Dear me." Even from my distance I could tell the man was laughing at me. That silent laughter is the worst kind. He had a mass of thick brown hair, rather rumpled by the wind, and the kind of aristocratic nose Robert would have sold his soul for. I won't discuss his eyes. No one should have such expressive eyes. "Do you think he's likely to do it soon?" the man asked. "It might be best if I removed my cravat first."

His mockery made me wish to remove his cravat myself and stuff it in his mouth. We seemed to be at an impasse. I had no way to hide my nakedness, and I was not going to climb out of the lagoon and walk straight up to where he sat to claim my clothes.

"Perhaps you think I'm some scullery maid or

washer woman, whom you may spy upon without fear of retribution,'' I said. ''Well, I'm not. I'm a gently born female who has a family to protect her, I assure you, sir. Now be off with you.'' I fluttered my fingers in a dismissive gesture, much as I believe a queen might use to rid herself of the unwanted presence of a servant.

My unwelcome visitor remained unmoved. He hid his twitching lips behind a large, long-fingered fist and studied me for some time. Finally he said, ''I had already determined that you were gently born by your clothes and your speech. As to your family protecting you . . . Well, I don't doubt their existence, but they aren't here and the view is so delightful I can scarcely tear myself away.''

He raised a languid hand to stall my protestations. ''Yes, I know. I am a most ungentlemanlike gentleman. It's been pointed out to me on more than one occasion, and I haven't the least urge to change, you know. Very stubborn of me, but there it is.''

My gaze went again, rather wistfully, to my clothes. ''How long do you intend to stay there?''

''Oh, I should think for some time yet. Though it's not the most comfortable seat I've ever had, it is certainly the most entertaining.''

''Have you no respect for my maidenly modesty?''

This time he did laugh, a deep and rather infectious sound that engulfed me and made me shiver with its vibrations. Dutch barked in sympathy with him, plodding about in a frenzy of excitement. So much for my throat-ripping dog.

It's very difficult to look haughty when your hair is hanging in wet curls around your face and your nude body is helplessly in view of some villain, but I did my best. I lifted my eyebrows and my nose went up with them, and I said, ''My family will be concerned if I don't arrive back at the house shortly.''

He shrugged his broad shoulders. The snug fit of his jacket was remarkable by our country standards. ''I have no intention of hindering your departure. In fact, I think it would be perfectly splendid if you would join me here on the rock. Please don't think I have any intention of harming you. You are perfectly safe with me.''

''Safe!'' I exclaimed. ''Only a rake and a libertine would behave so odiously. I fear for my very life.''

''Come, come,'' he said soothingly. ''I have the greatest admiration for you. You aren't the first woman I've seen naked. I shall be perfectly capable of resisting any wayward impulse to ravish you. There's something positively captivating about outraged innocence in a perfectly proportioned frame.'' He looked up at the sky, a small frown drawing his brows together. ''I think it must be the artist in me.''

''You must think me the greatest fool on earth to believe you are an artist. You're nothing more than a Peeping Tom.''

He sighed and thrust out his hands, palms up. ''You have misunderstood me again. I simply meant that your beauty touches my soul.''

''Humph,'' I snorted. ''More like it touches your . . .''

His grin tempted me to finish my sentence, but I had no intention of walking farther down *that* path. Robert had already told me my tongue was a little free in these matters. Though why I should feign a maidenly lack of knowledge is beyond my understanding. After all, men already know about these things, a great deal more than I do. Would my total ignorance enhance their knowledge somehow?

Well, that's neither here nor there. This fellow continued to observe me, a wicked gleam in his eyes. I wasn't able to cover myself, because I needed my hands to keep afloat. With sudden inspiration, I re-

membered a day when Robert and I were children and
had a splashing match. There was a certain way you
could hold your hand that would send the water a great
distance. We'd even gotten our clothes, lying on the
rocks, soaking wet. Which would happen again, no
doubt, if I tried to spray him. Still, it was worth that
difficulty. I paddled a little closer to where he sat,
which made him eye me quizzingly.

With a whoop I began to spray him, large arcs of
water curving out of the lagoon and neatly landing
right on his chest. Much to my surprise, he began to
laugh, rather than showing any annoyance or trying to
get out of range of my spray. Really, it was too exas-
perating of him.

Suddenly he held up his hand, fiercely whispering,
"Stop!"

I paid no attention to him. It satisfied my sense of
fair play to at least inconvenience the fellow. So he
leapt down to the edge of the water and glared at me.
He was intimidating in that pose, much as my father
had been when he was alive and intended that I should
obey him. This man was perhaps more threatening because he was a stranger and I had no way of knowing
what kind of a temper he had. I instantly fell still, and
then I could hear it, too.

There was the distant sound of voices, coming from
somewhere outside the enclosed space. One of the men
sounded very much like our estate manager, Roderick
Hughes. The last thing on earth I wanted was for him
to find me there! The poor old fellow would stick his
spoon in the wall for sure. And if it was Cousin Bret
with him, that would be too mortifying. That con-
ceited numskull would never let me forget it if he
caught me swimming naked.

My countenance must have given me away. The tall
man frowned and whispered, "No doubt they've found
my horse. I'll distract them. You get out of here as

soon as you can, for God's sake. But not before that gown dries, mind you. I know what a damped petticoat does to the female figure, and you don't want to be passing by all your neighbors in that condition.''

He turned away without a further glance at me. I was grateful to him, for this small service. Not that I was going to thank him, mind you.

He didn't even bother to remove his boots to wade through the narrow passage. But it was several minutes before I heard his voice on the other side. Perhaps he'd managed to elude them until he was some distance from the entrance, because his voice sounded quite distant when he spoke.

''Now, now, there's no need to lay a hand on me, my dear fellow,'' he protested, in a mild drawl that almost made me laugh.

Cousin Bret's voice was much more penetrating. ''What do you mean by this intrusion? Our lands are clearly marked. I've a mind to send for a constable.''

''Have you? Well, I'm sure you must do precisely as you wish. For my part, I'll be heading on up to the manor house, if you'll be so kind as to return my horse to me.''

''And how do I know this is your horse?'' Cousin Bret asked, an obvious insult intended by his tone. ''I've never laid eyes on you before in my life, so don't pretend that you are known at the manor.''

''No, Robert's not there to vouch for me,'' the stranger admitted, ''but I daresay that won't matter. I have his commission in my pocket. No, no, I have no intention of showing it to you. It's addressed quite clearly to Mrs. Ryder and I have every confidence that you are not she.''

He knew Robert! Oh, God. I would never hear the end of this. First he would tell my mother—for my own good, of course; they always say that—and then he would tell Robert. I climbed out of the pond and hopped up to the ledge where my gown lay, wet and bedraggled. Not that it made any difference. Dutch blinked sleepily up at me from his spot on the rock.

From the distance I heard Mr. Hughes speak for the first time. "It's a fine horse you have here, sir. If I can be helping you with directions to the manor, you've only to ask. Was it a shortcut you was intending?"

Good old Hughes. No one could be better at ferreting out information in the politest possible way. He sounded so respectful, compared with my cousin. But then, most everyone did. Cousin Bret had managed to offend just about everyone since he arrived for his annual summer visit. He was far too old at twenty-one to keep coming around here each summer as though he were still a child. I don't know why Robert hadn't warned him off this year. Papa would have been disgusted by the way Cousin Bret had turned out, all bossy and proud. There was very little to interest him at Hastings, except perhaps my sister. And even Amanda wasn't odd enough to be taken in by Cousin Bret.

The stranger was explaining to Hughes that the glimmer of water on such an oppressive day had indeed tempted him to cut across country. "Apollo was in need of a drink, to say nothing of myself. I must have fallen asleep in the shade."

"That sun's a killer today," Hughes agreed. "Good thing your horse didn't wander off."

"Oh, Apollo's not in the habit of doing that," the man assured him. I could hear the creak of the saddle as he swung himself up. "If you'll just point me in the direction of the manor . . ."

As the hoofbeats receded, I listened for Cousin Bret's comment, but he was strangely silent. Mr. Hughes said only, "Fine-looking fellow. Must have met Mr. Robert in London. Perhaps we can look forward to Mr. Robert paying us a visit soon."

"Not likely," Cousin Bret sneered.

And I feared he was right, much as I hated to admit it. Robert seemed to have lost all taste for the country life. I tugged on my damp shift, which felt clammy against my skin. The hot sun would dry everything out in no time, but the thought brought little solace when I thought of what lay in store for me at home. I tied my rumpled bonnet securely under my chin and carried by shoes and stockings to the narrow entrance. The basset waddled down off the rocks and splashed into the water behind me. We made quite a procession heading back to Hastings.

·2·

I managed to get all the way to the house without seeing anyone. There's a kitchen garden just off the pantry that I was in the habit of frequenting when I was a child. Mrs. Cooper is still very pleased whenever I show up in her domain. Though I must admit that she looked rather taken aback by my rumpled appearance.

"Your sister will have a good laugh if she sees you, Miss Catherine," she said as she wiped her big red hands on the sacking apron she wore. "No more's the wonder. Your bonnet might have been run over by a carriage, by the looks of it."

"Very nearly," I quipped. Mrs. Cooper does not allow any of the dogs in her kitchen, not even Dutch, so he whimpered outside as I shut the door behind me. "I'll have one of those plums if you'd be so good as to allow me."

"Just one, then up to your room to change. There's company." She said this with a meaningful toss of her head. "A very presentable young man, Milly says."

Milly thinks just about every young man is very presentable, but in this instance I happened to agree, so far as his looks were concerned.

"Who is he?" I asked in a very casual way.

Mrs. Cooper frowned slightly, trying to remember. "Let me see. It sounded like a field, I think. Meddows. That was it. Sir John Meddows. Acquainted with

Mr. Robert, he is. Had a letter for the missus from your brother. She was that glad to get it, what with him being so absentminded about his family.''

A distinct disapproval colored her speech, though I can assure you that Robert is her favorite. Everyone is so disappointed that Robert has taken the country in dislike and developed a positive affection for the city. I remember the first time he visited London. He was disgusted then with the noise and the cost of everything. But that was when he was seven, and he has changed a great deal since then.

''Well, I believe I feel the headache coming on.'' No reason to run straight into the lion's den, so far as I could see. ''Perhaps I'll just lie down a bit. If I miss Robert's friend it will be a great shame, of course, but this heat is awful and I shouldn't like to become sick from it.''

''You don't *look* sick.'' Her dark eyes ranged from my rosy face to my dusty feet. ''I'm sure your mama would want you to join them, if you feel at all up to it.''

''Perhaps in a while,'' I said in a failing voice. I shouldn't have done that. Mrs. Cooper is no one's fool. Her eyes sharpened and I could see she was about to question me, so I skipped past her and palmed one of the purple plums. ''Just quizzing you.'' I laughed as I bounded for the back stairs. ''But the sun does beat straight through a thin cotton bonnet . . .''

By the time I'd reached my room, I was very curious about this friend of Robert's. It seemed suspicious to me that he had arrived when Robert was away. And it was certainly not at all likely that a legitimate fellow would have sat and stared at a naked woman swimming on Hastings land. In fact, the more I thought about it, the more I became convinced that he would not dare tell on me. After all, I would come right back with his own improper behavior, and my family was obliged to believe me. They would have no trouble believing that I had found a private bathing pond and would do something so unconventional as to swim naked there. Not that I'd done anything of the sort before, but they'd seen me through plenty of scrapes.

I took off the yellow gown and dropped it on the floor, noticing as I did so that the sun had turned my skin pink all over. Mercy! But no one was going to know that if I wore a gown that covered most of me, as the lot of them did, since Amanda was forever involving herself in my wardrobe. Mama was convinced that Amanda had impeccable taste, as well as a sense of decorum that was entirely denied me. It was but one of many trials Amanda created in my life.

When I had dipped a cloth in the ewer and rinsed off my face, I felt a great deal better. I was even convinced that I looked rather attractive in this flushed state, and the idea began to grow in me that I would join Mama and this stranger after all. Let him try to stare me down! It was he who should be put out of countenance by my arrival, though somehow I doubted he would be.

Choosing a gown was easy. In the wardrobe there were only pale pastels and whites, dresses that I had acquired for my one Season in London and that I'd been wearing for the two years since. None of them seemed particularly interesting to me by now—few of them ever had—but at least the soft green with the draped bodice would still be considered a bit out of the ordinary. (Amanda hadn't been there when we chose it.) Green has a way of bringing out the color of my eyes and is a superior shade to wear against my auburn hair.

Without my maid's help I couldn't have gotten downstairs in under an hour because the water had tangled my hair so desperately. Milly is a good girl, though prone to ask awkward questions, such as

"However did you get your hair in such a rat's nest, Miss Catherine?" I palmed her off with some absent-minded excuse, because I was eager to hear her impression of our visitor.

"He's ever so handsome, miss," she told me with a little sway of her shoulders. "And very well spoken. A friend of Mr. Robert's, I believe. Sir John Meddows, his card said. A baronet. Do you think Miss Amanda would like to marry a baronet?"

Her question caught me completely off-guard. "Amanda? What has she to do with anything?"

"Why, miss, didn't I say? The gentleman caught a glimpse of her in the garden as he rode in, and he was so struck by her beauty that he sat astride his horse for a full five minutes staring at her. I know, because I saw it all from the drawing-room window. Proper stunned, he was." Milly sighed at this example of the most romantic of experiences. She's a great believer in love at first sight, our Milly. There isn't a footman who's been added to our staff who wasn't declared struck dumb by his instant passion for one of the parlor maids.

"How very rude of him to stare." Really, the man had no finesse at all. Amanda is indeed as pretty as a picture, if you're inclined to admire the fainting, placid-angel type. All that blond hair peeking out from under her bonnets, curling down her back. No doubt she had heard his horse and was posing for him, in the event it was Jeremy Woods from over to Newmarket.

Milly was affronted by my declaration. "Nothing of the sort, Miss Catherine! He was afluster with apology when Miss Amanda looked up and caught him at it. Made her the prettiest speech you ever heard."

He certainly hadn't made *me* a pretty speech, the villain. Now I was getting a better idea of his vast duplicity. And that made me impatient to join my family. He might be trying to take advantage of them, even now.

"That will do, thank you, Milly," I said as she pushed in one more pin to hold up the mass of my hair. She loves to part it in the center with two wings over my forehead, and the bulk of it twisted into a flaming knot at the top of my head. Amanda professes to be very sorry for me for the color of my hair, but I would far rather have this glowing chestnut shade than her pale, insipid yellow.

They were all in the gold drawing room when I reached it: Mama, Amanda, and Sir John Meddows. I didn't realize at the pond that he was so large a man, quite six feet tall, I would say, with impressive shoulders. When he rose to greet me, there was not even a flicker of recognition in his eyes.

"And this is Robert's other sister?" he said, stepping forward to grasp my hand. "How delighted I am to meet you. Your brother is not so forthcoming as I had thought, since he neglected to mention how lovely were the three ladies awaiting him here at Hastings."

"How do you do, Sir John?" I withdrew my hand instantly from his warm clasp. It was too much, reminding me of him sitting there by the water, observing my naked body. I could hardly be so casual as he, though I eyed him quite boldly and with my most haughty expression. Which is not particularly haughty, I am told, after all. "What has brought you to our neighborhood?"

He smiled pleasantly and waited until I had seated myself before taking his place beside Mama on the sofa. "Your brother Robert assures me that the best-bred horses in England are to be found at Hinchly Farms, not five miles from here. I want to find a pair for myself, and he begged me to look out a new pair for him as well. Apparently his old grays aren't so lively any longer."

Robert's grays! They were Papa's grays, to everyone

at Hastings. And we expected them to live forever. "You must see that he returns the grays here, when he replaces them," I insisted. "We're all very fond of them."

"So your mother was telling me." He crossed his legs and folded his large hands on his lap, though he didn't look at all like someone who made a habit of morning calls or visiting ladies for tea. Every athletic bone in his body must have cried out to be away from there.

Such a muscular calf as he had! Lord, I don't think one of the fellows in the area could compete with it. And yet, I didn't remember meeting him when I was in London for my Season. All the gudgeons I met then were the worst of the dandies, with their perfumed handkerchiefs and their dainty airs. No wonder I didn't take! Who would want to take with a bunch of pinks of the *ton* like that? I couldn't help wondering where Robert had found this man.

"Sir John was telling us that he comes from Hampshire," Mama informed me. "He has an estate there that Robert has visited on several occasions."

There was a certain amount of accusation in her voice. After all, Robert hadn't been to visit us for quite a while.

"Short visits. And I'm so close to London," Sir John almost apologized for the occasions.

"What sort of pair do you need?" I asked. One of my passions is driving, but I've been warned that on no account am I to mention it to strangers, and only to our usual company if they happen to bring the subject up. "Do you drive a curricle?"

His eyes looked amused, as though I'd said something precocious. "I do. One of my own design, which is a little more hazardous than the usual, I fear. It's balance is a trifle finer, and therefore it's more prone to overset."

"I should like to see it," I said, noting that Mama's eyes had narrowed in my direction.

"Perhaps someday you shall. My groom is bringing it along after me; he had to have the shaft repaired in Littlebury." He turned to Mama. "Which reminds me. I've spoken for a room in Cambridge at the White Horse, which seemed a perfectly acceptable hostelry. Will they take good care of my horses?"

"Of course they will!" I asserted at the same time Mama exclaimed, "We wouldn't think of letting you stay at an inn when we have the largest, most comfortable house in the world, and with a staff of stable fellows who could care for your animals far better than any public inn. Really, I'm surprised that Robert wouldn't have told you that you were to stay with us."

Amanda and I both stared at Mama. It wasn't at all like her to make this kind of offer to a comparative stranger. In many ways, she's a shy woman, as well as being eccentric. Or perhaps she's shy because she's eccentric. In any case, we were surprised, but I think not displeased, that she offered to house the fellow. Amanda because of his dashing looks, no doubt, but me because I was intent on keeping an eye on him. Warning signals were going off in my head, for I was sure there was more to his visit than met the eye.

Sir John accepted the invitation with becoming hesitation. "If you're sure you have the room. I should hate to put you out." That sort of thing. But I could tell that he'd never intended to stay at the White Horse at all. Though perhaps he meant to put his pair up there when they arrived.

"You must bring your luggage straightaway," Mama urged him. "You'll have the blue bedchamber, next to Robert's room in the east wing. I think you'll like the prospect from the windows. Several of the church spires in Cambridge are visible. You didn't by chance go up to Cambridge, did you?"

"No, ma'am. I'm an Oxford man myself."

I wouldn't have taken him to be an educated soul at all. Certainly not of the sort who read Latin in the original and have long, pithy discussions on Sydney Smith's essays in the *Edinburgh Review*. Papa would have been able to unmask the fellow in short order if he tried to pretend to such learning. But Papa was gone, alas.

"I could show you around the grounds, if you like," Amanda offered. "We have some delightful walks at Hastings."

It's a wonder she didn't expire on the spot, putting herself forward that way. I studied her closely and saw the tint of a blush in her cheeks. She must have felt like a hussy, making such a daring proposal. Ah, it was clear enough that she was taken with the rascal.

Mama beamed on the two of them. You would have thought I wasn't there at all. Just to throw them into a little disarray, I asked, "Where has Cousin Bret gotten to, I wonder? Usually he's hanging about Amanda in the afternoons."

The color in my sister's cheeks rose even higher. "It is no such thing," she declared hotly. "I understand Cousin Bretford is out with the estate manager, gathering a little information about crops and such."

Amanda knows absolutely nothing about "crops and such." Nor does Robert. And I'm afraid I'm not all that knowledgeable myself, though certainly a great deal more than the two of them put together.

Sir John laughed. "I hope you have no intention of interesting me in the crops when we make our little excursion," he teased. "The grounds and the woods are much more to my taste."

I was sure of it. He probably thought he could get Amanda among the trees and ravish her. Well, perhaps not ravish her, but kiss her at least. I could see how his gaze remained on her full, pouty mouth. Why does a man think it famous to spend time with a pouty woman? My understanding of men is of the smallest, I daresay, but I have no respect for the ones who want a woman they can wrap about their fingers.

That may be because no one could wrap me around his finger.

Sir John agreed that he would like nothing better than to be taken through the grounds by Amanda—when he returned with his portmanteau and his carriage from the inn later that evening. Would he be with us to dine, Mama asked. Yes, he would certainly be here by then, he assured her. As he took his leave, he smiled kindly upon each of us, but I thought there was a slight twist to his lips when he looked at me, a rather sardonic twist.

"I look forward to seeing you again soon," he said. To my ears there was an undercurrent of mockery to his voice. No one else seemed to notice.

I could hardly wait until he was out of the house before begging to see Robert's letter. Mama dug it out of the deep pocket in her dress and straightened it out before handing it to me. "Your brother speaks very highly of Sir John," she remarked. "I hope you will be pleasant to him."

"Pleasant? Of course I shall be pleasant to him. When am I anything but pleasant to anyone?"

Amanda tittered and Mama gave a little puff of a laugh. Where they get this impression that I am rude or unfriendly, I can't imagine, but I decided to pay no heed to them. The first order of business was to discover what information I could on this provocative stranger. Robert's letter wasn't much help:

My dearest Mama,

This letter will introduce Sir John Meddows to you. John is a great friend of mine, and an excellent judge of horseflesh. I've asked him to look out a pair for me for my phaeton while he's in your area. He knew of the Overview stables, but not of Hinchly Farms, so he has a treat in store for himself. I've warned him not to let Catherine hoodwink him into buying *her* favorite animal, as she's done to me so many times!

And he should be grateful to me, the cad. I've *never* led him astray.

My best to you and my sisters. Your letters are always welcome, though I'm afraid I'm a poor correspondent myself. Perhaps I'll come down for opening day, but probably not. There's much better shooting at Chelverton. Your loving son,

Robert

It was still more than a month until shooting season began and we'd hoped Robert would come down for Public Day in mid-July. He'd never missed one before, but then, Papa had been alive for all the others. Last year's had been canceled because we were in mourning and I think all the neighbors and servants were looking forward to this one. I sighed and handed the letter back to Mama.

"Have you asked him about coming down for Public Day?" I asked.

"I've mentioned it in every letter for the last month," she said with some asperity, "and, as you see, he makes no mention of it. Whatever can have gotten into the boy?"

It was a rhetorical question. Not that any of us knew the answer. It occurred to me that Sir John might, though. And perhaps that was what Mama had in mind when she asked him to stay. Very clever of her. Keeping an eye on him would be my primary concern.

I could manage that with a little perseverance. Sir John might not be willing to listen to my opinions about horses, but I was established, if only to his amusement, as the knowledgeable one in the family, and he might well be obliged to take me with him. In fact, I would see that he did.

When I went upstairs to dress for dinner, I insisted that Milly do something different with my hair. It wasn't to impress our visitor; it was from a distinct fatigue with my usual style. Milly managed to coax my rambunctious curls to remain tamed at my temples, and the long tresses to stay down in back with merely a string of pearls capturing them at my neck. A very satisfactory solution, something the maidens in London might have done well to copy, I thought.

Amanda was green with envy. "What have you done to your hair?" she demanded in that shrill voice she is reduced to by hysteria. "You can't wear it like that! You've let Milly get carried away. I tell you that girl ought to find herself a position as a hairdresser."

"I think it looks quite nice," I said, waving aside her concerns. "And yours does, too, Amanda. I don't think you've worn it so fluffed out in the last two years. Is this the newest style in *Le Beau Monde*?"

"That has nothing to do with it. I wanted to wear it in the usual way, but Mama insisted that her woman could make me look a good two years older by working with it." It was hard to tell whether this distressed or pleased her by the simpering expression she wore. She straightened the lace fichu that closely guarded her modesty. "Mama says gentlemen don't always pay attention to the youngest woman in a gathering, if she hasn't been out in London. And while we all know that I should have been out but for Papa's death, well, a stranger wouldn't know that. So it seemed prudent to enhance my age by just this trifle."

"It suits admirably," I complimented her. "You'll have Sir John eating out of your hand in no time."

"Catherine! How can you say such a thing!"

"Never mind!" I dashed down the stairs away from her protestations. "He'll be here soon. Don't let your distress raise your color too high."

I don't know why I can't restrain myself from teasing her. She's such an easy target. Rather unworthy, actually. I had made it to the hall when there was a strong hammering on the front door. Our butler, Williams, is country-bred and consequently rather stiff with some of the more exalted personages who appear at our door. Without so much as a flicker of his eyes, he ushered the baronet into the house, but I got the distinct impression, nonetheless, that he disapproved of Sir John. Our visitor wore a driving coat with more than a dozen capes; we dress more conservatively than that in the country.

Behind Sir John I could see the curricle being taken away toward the stables. It was indeed a magnificent sight. Glistening black with red trim and yellow wheels. His groom held a steady hand on the reins as a pair of perfectly matched chestnuts strutted off down the drive.

"Think you could handle it?" Sir John asked me as he handed his gloves to Williams.

It was an impertinent question, and meant to depress my pretensions to some familiarity with horses. "Of course I could handle it," I said stoutly, though I wasn't at all sure because it had been more than a year since I drove Robert's. But Sir John had put my back up and I wasn't going to admit it. I have always taken some pride in my riding and driving skills.

His brows rose almost to his thick brown hair. "Ah, I see. Your brother told me you have some faith in yourself as a whipster. But I very much fear it would be remiss of me to allow you an opportunity with my curricle. As I mentioned, it's an unstable vehicle."

The footman was bringing two portmanteaus into the house and I noted that they were large enough to serve Sir John for quite a stay. Williams asked, in his roughly formal voice, if Sir John's man would be coming, and our visitor admitted that he would, in a day or two. I received the distinct impression that Sir John was settling in for a considerable stay. And I wondered why. And how I felt about that.

·3·

We sat down five to dinner. Mrs. Cooper had outdone herself with the entrees—lobster cutlets and beef palates *à la italienne*—but I found myself more interested in the conversation than the food. Cousin Bret had treated Sir John with a certain coolness when they met in the drawing room before dinner, and I was eager to see how the baronet handled my cousin's sniping over the meal. Cousin Bret prides himself on his ability to carry on a distinguished discourse with even the lowliest and least intelligent of his fellow human beings—which is just about everyone except himself—and his condescension was a matter of humor within the family. I didn't think Sir John would see it in quite the same light. Their exchange went something like this:

Cousin Bret: I hear we're to have the honor of your company for a brief visit, Sir John.

Sir John *(smiling at my mother):* Mrs. Ryder has been so kind as to invite me to make my stay at Hastings while I search out some carriage horses for Robert and myself. I understand there are several excellent breeders in the area.

Cousin Bret *(with a smug laugh):* Oh, I doubt if they can match the quality of the breeders in my own county. Somerset, you know. Nothing is so suitable for horses as the rich pasturage and sweet-smelling air there.

Sir John: You surprise me. I had no idea Somerset was famed for its horse breeding. Now, I suppose that will mean that my search here will take longer than I'd anticipated, Mrs. Ryder. Perhaps I should put up at the inn after all.

Mother *(understanding that he was only teasing):* Not at all! You are to stay here just as long as it is convenient for you, Sir John. Any friend of Robert's . . .

Sir John: How kind of you! I must admit that I am tempted. *(He glances with favor upon my sister.)* But we shall see, we shall see.

Cousin Bret *(with a sneer):* You must take my Cousin Catherine's advice in choosing your pair. I'm sure she'll be more than willing to give you the benefit of her knowledge.

Me: Sir John has already made it clear that he thinks it unlikely I know anything about horses.

Sir John *(with a pretense at surprise):* Have I? My dear Miss Ryder, I'm sure you must have mistaken me. Even your dear brother mentioned the matter before I left London.

Cousin Bret *(interrupting the indignant remark I'd intended to make):* Yes, indeed. Cousin Catherine has cultivated that most pressing of the ladylike arts: judging horseflesh. Why, I remember when she was a child and hung around the stables all day . . .

Mama: I think we're due for even hotter weather, don't you, Sir John? Amanda will show you some of the cool spots in our garden, if the heat becomes unbearable.

* * *

And so forth. It was really a most unsatisfactory meal, with Cousin Bret taunting me, or trying to give Sir John a set-down. Mama managed to keep me from telling my cousin what I thought of him, something I do on a fairly regular basis, but Sir John didn't even seem to notice Cousin Bret's pinpricks. Which, of course, infuriated my cousin. He's not used to being found of so little consequence. And Sir John managed to do it in such a polite manner that even my cousin could not have faulted him for his behavior.

Much as I detest Cousin Bret, I have to admit that I didn't like our visitor coming off so well. Both Mama and Amanda were immensely impressed with him, though, I could tell. Most unfortunate. I could scarcely manage the gosling in the third course for worrying about it.

Mama looked particularly splendid in a gown she hadn't worn in more than a year, and one that was, if the truth were told, a little too elegant for the evening. Sir John didn't seem to notice. I was delighted when Cousin Bret excused himself from joining us in the gold room. He always made me feel that he scorned Mama's choice of outfits. Mama's style of dressing has never been quite in the ordinary mode, but that is no business of Cousin Bret's.

The gold room is the most impressive room at Hastings. A single cube room of thirty feet in each dimension, it is the untouched work of Inigo Jones. There is a chimneypiece of Italian marble with great swags of fruits and flowers carved in wood above it, painted white and gilded in different shades of gold.

Dotted about the huge space are gilt and red velvet settees and fragile chairs and elaborate mirrors by Chippendale, which were all designed just for this room. The coved ceilings are particularly ornate and all around the room are panels meant to hold family portraits. But we Ryders have a penchant for sporting scenes, so only a few portraits grace the area, above the mantel and near the door. Mama busied herself adjusting the fire screen, though there was no fire on the grate. This was usually a sign of agitation in her.

"Have you been to Robert's lodgings in the city?" she asked soon after Sir John had taken the seat she indicated beside Amanda on the sofa.

"On many occasions," he replied. Though he sounded open and aboveboard, I detected a trace of reserve—or caution—in his eyes.

"We opened the house in Grosvenor Street when Catherine came out, but Robert didn't want to live there when he went up to London this time," Mama explained.

"Far too large for him, of course. Our place in Berkeley Square is the same, but my mother makes periodic excursions to town, so there is always a minimal staff. Robert indicated that your house in town had been let for a while. Perhaps ever since Miss Ryder was presented in London? I'm certain I missed that occasion."

His subtle amusement made me wish to stomp on his toes, but I merely lifted my nose a fraction of an inch. Mama ignored his reference to my Season.

"Yes, the house is let and has been for over a year, but I daresay it could be made available to him at any time. In fact, I urged him to take it the last time the lease was up for renewal."

Sir John rested a hand along the back of the settee. "Robert is very comfortably situated in his rooms on Mount Street. The place is large enough to be comfortable and small enough for his man and one female servant to take care of it with no trouble. Perhaps one day you'll come up to see it for yourself."

"Perhaps," Mama said vaguely. She fingered the lace ruffle on her sleeve with nervous fingers. "I've never quite understood what it is young men do when they live in London. How do they occupy their time?"

His broad smile was almost rakish. "Oh, there are a thousand things for a young blood to do, my dear ma'am. Riding in the park and visiting with one's friends, the balls, the parties, the shops, the clubs. Almost more than a fellow can fit into a day."

"But that's all play!" Mama protested. "When my husband went up to town he at least had business to occupy much of his time. The diversions were of great interest, of course, but they were offset with a certain amount of honest effort." She rose to pace the room, adjusting a picture frame with a *tsk* as she passed. It was far more crooked afterward. Amanda and I glanced at each other and looked away.

Mama continued. "When we were in town with Catherine for her Season, there was so much to prepare for, just for her introduction to society. I suppose one could look on it all as very frivolous, but it is serious business for any family to see their daughters well established."

I felt mortified by this discussion. As though I were a task they meant to accomplish! And failed, at that.

Sir John eyed me with interest. "It's a challenge," he said, his lips twitching ever so slightly. "I'm surprised Miss Ryder didn't carry off half a dozen hearts with her."

"She did, she did! Only she would accept none of them. Not that I blame her," Mama admitted. "You've never seen such a disappointing group of suitors. Perhaps it was the war. Or just not a particularly pleasant Season because of the dreary weather, but they were all spotty young men or gouty old men, certainly no one of a caliber to win Catherine's heart. And I assure you I do not look for marriage where there is no attachment. My Catherine will not be pushed to wed for the convenience of her family."

She spoke so vehemently that Amanda now looked mortified. This agitation and plain speaking are one of Mama's eccentricities. There are other, more serious ones, which will become evident as my story progresses. Her distress about matrimony was not because of any circumstance of her own. Mama was not forced into marrying my father. No such thing. She was dearly in love with him from the day she first saw him until the day he died. I sometimes think that is why . . . But I get ahead of myself.

"I'm sure Miss Ryder would discover a most suitable *parti* if she were to venture upon the town again," he suggested, with just that inflection that indicates "this is the polite thing to say" and not that he really meant it. "And hasn't Miss Amanda come out yet, then?" His eyes sought and held my sister's.

"She would have, except that Mr. Ryder died only two months before her Season was to begin. Just over a year ago." Mama frequently has to dab at her eyes when she says this sort of thing, but that night she merely held her head a little higher and went on. "Our year of mourning is past now and it is time we saw to Amanda's presentation. Not in London until the fall Little Season, of course, but here, perhaps, on our Public Day. We used to give a ball of sorts, country-style, but quite a pleasant affair. I'm sure we could do that again."

Amanda blushed with pleasure and with the attention this questionable stranger was giving her. His eyes continued to linger on her countenance. "It sounds a most delightful solution," he said. "Perhaps Robert would come down for it."

"That is just what I was thinking," Mama admitted. "I am convinced that he would be more likely to do so if you were to be here for the affair. It's only three weeks' distant. You could stay until then."

"You're good to include me, but I really cannot feel I should impose on your hospitality for such a lengthy period of time."

"Do consider it. I realize our entertainments aren't half so elegant as any you would come upon in town, but I do have my two charming daughters to tempt your interest."

"Strong inducement, indeed."

By the pond, there had been a dangerous, rakish light in his eyes. But now he sat at his ease, meek as a lamb, looking just the sort of fellow Amanda could set her heart on and Mama could trust. I did not for a moment believe this was his true nature, and I was determined to prove it before he managed to disrupt our whole household.

The night was clear and warm and he suggested a walk with the three of us in the gardens. Mama declined but insisted that Amanda and I accompany him. We each wrapped a shawl about our bare shoulders and stepped out into the refreshing evening air. Sir John gallantly offered an arm to each and Amanda coyly placed three fingers on his. I gripped his arm firmly, and was startled by the strength of it. Of necessity I ignored his sardonic expression.

As we walked along, his head inclined frequently to Amanda's side. "Tell me what gardening you do," he said. "My mother is such an avid gardener that I know a deal more about garden flowers than field crops."

Fortunately for my sister, she knows a bit about nemesia and delphinium, rambler roses and centaurea. The entire walk through the hedged garden is perfumed by stocks, a fact that has been pointed out to me any number of times, though I couldn't distinguish a stock from a sweet pea to save my life. Not that Sir John asked me to, or paid the least attention to my occasional quips.

Though Amanda pointed to various kinds of flowers, and Sir John dutifully regarded them, his gaze was scarcely restricted to the flower beds. He managed to take in every gravel path and half-hidden succession house as we walked. He was as inquisitive as a three-year-old.

"Where does that path lead?" He pointed down the far border to where a gate let out into the home wood.

My sister acted as though he had suggested an assignation to her. She dipped her head and peered at him through her long, golden eyelashes. "Just into a glade in the woods. There's no horse trail in that direction. The glade is infrequently visited these days, since the path is rather overgrown."

"That won't deter us," he remarked, with a long gaze into her blue eyes. "I can tell you're not the kind of woman who's put off by a little unruly grass."

"No, no, of course not," she agreed in a hopelessly breathless voice.

I never thought Amanda would be so gullible. This man was having her on, no doubt about it. His behavior was almost a caricature of a man infatuated—and he'd only known her for five hours! But there would be no convincing Amanda of it. She expected men to pay attention to her and probably fantasized that one day such a handsome fellow would come along and fall madly in love with her at first sight.

The gold tassels on his Hessians swung jauntily as he walked, and Amanda watched them in sheer fascination. I could practically feel her awe. None of the gentlemen in our neighborhood owned Hessians like that, or as I mentioned previously, coats that clung to broad shoulders like a second skin. I wondered what Amanda would do if Sir John tried to kiss her. I'll bet she's never been kissed, though she's allowed enough young men to dangle after her. Whereas I . . . Well, my story is a little different.

I should admit that Amanda never encouraged Cousin Bret to dangle after her. No amount of wooing on his part could determine her to pay the least notice of him. Which is why I couldn't fault her judgment entirely. I was convinced she was playing with dangerous stuff if she encouraged Sir John, though.

"And where are the stables?" he was inquiring. "I wonder if you would mind very much, my dear Miss Amanda, if we were to just make a brief stop there. I'd like to see that my horses and groom are settled in."

No one cared a whit if I wanted to go there or not!

Naturally we went to the stables. "Is there a direct path from here to the house?" he asked.

Amanda assured him that there was.

"If I'm late coming in of an evening, will I have any difficulty getting in the house?"

"Oh, I shouldn't think so," she said. "One of the footmen is on duty all night in the front hall."

"Perhaps there's another way in, that would be less disruptive to the household," he suggested.

"Well, I'm not sure." Amanda looked across his wide chest to consult me. "Is there, Catherine?"

As if I were going to tell this stranger about our arrangements! "I don't see any problem with him using the front entrance, just as everyone else does. That is, after all, the purpose of having a footman available."

Sir John was not satisfied with my answer. He frowned down at me. "Surely your brother Robert didn't always wish to pass a footman's inspection late at night. I've noticed there are back stairs that must come almost directly from the rear of the house. I suspect there's a key to that door hidden somewhere outside. Just the sort of thing we'd do at my home, you know."

"I'm sure I wouldn't know," I sniffed. "Perhaps you aren't so concerned with security at your home."

"Why, I believe you're right," Amanda exclaimed, clapping her hands as though she'd just made the most famous discovery. "Robert hated to come in by the front entrance when he'd been . . . off with his friends and out late. I'm sure he kept a key in a compartment of the bird-feeder in the kitchen garden. Let's go look for it!''

''Capital idea!''

Honestly, the man sounded more like a burglar than a houseguest.

By the time we'd checked on his horses and uncovered a rusting old key, I was irritated beyond anything. He was encouraging my sister's obvious infatuation; in fact, he seemed to know precisely how to act to enhance it. Yet I would have sworn he wasn't quite the man she surmised—charming, thoughtful, considerate, honorable. That devilish demeanor he'd displayed at the pond might be in hiding now, but it certainly wasn't a figment of my imagination.

The long and short of it was that I didn't trust Sir John one inch. I decided to set a trap for him that night, by tying a thread across his door. If the thread was broken in the morning, I would know that he had left his room that night, and the next night I'd be on the watch for him. It was the saddest thing that my sleep would be ruined, but there are some sacrifices one must make.

I set about my task soon after everyone had retired. When I stood in the darkened hall and strung the thread from the shining brass doorknob to the elaborate sconce beside the door frame, I could hear the man still moving around in his room and then the protest of the bed as he climbed onto it.

His room, which was only around the corner from mine, had a delightful canopied bed that was rather a conversation piece in our family. There were rumors that several illustrious people had slept in it—and one of them had carved his initials, like a common schoolboy! My father had picked it up at an auction five years previously. We weren't the sort of family the great and near-great visited as a common occurrence. Though we would become a little more prominent when Robert came into the earldom. But I digress. I'll explain that anon.

Sir John was a large man, but the bed was enormous and I heard his murmur of approbation as he stretched out on the comfortable down mattress. If he decided to get up in the night and wander out of his room, he wouldn't notice the thread, since it would break with the greatest of ease. I would have chosen something different if I'd wanted a different result, like locking him in his room! It would come to that only in an emergency.

Exhausted from the excitemusts of the day, I crept back to my room. My body remained pink and warm from the sun. Seeing it in the glass served to remind me of Sir John's villainy and I blushed to think of his view. Well, I would repay him for his misdeeds in time.

Dutch sleeps in my room, at the foot of my bed, and when I arose in the early-dawn light, I nearly stepped on him. He gave a yelp of terror and padded off to a safe corner while I slipped a dressing gown over my nightdress. My eyes were half-shut with sleep and my hair was tousled from my pillow. I had decided to climb back in bed when I was finished. I would just slip down the hall and around the corner to check the thread before there was any chance that Sir John awoke.

I knew every spot in the hall that makes the slightest squeak. We used to wander around a lot when we were children—against the express wishes of our nanny, of course. So I was able to creep along quite silently to Sir John's door. The thread I'd used was black, and in the dimness I couldn't see if it was there. I reached out to run a finger along the frame, to feel for it.

"My, my," a voice whispered close by me. "I had

no idea the mermaid was given to early-morning visits, or I would certainly have stayed in my bed.''

His voice had so startled me that I literally felt my heart leap in my chest and knock against my ribs. I found myself flattened against his door, cowering away from him, but thank goodness my voice did not let me down. "So there you are," I whispered back fiercely. "I knew you would be out during the night on some nefarious activity, and I've caught you!"

"My dear girl, you have done nothing of the sort. And if you insist on a rendezvous with a male houseguest, I really think I should advise you to dress a little more, ah, glamorously. It's all well for a man to realize that his dearest may look a bit rumpled in the morning, but he doesn't really want to see it, if you take my meaning."

"I did not come here for a rendezvous! I came to check the . . ."

"What? You came to check the what?" he asked, his eyes shining with amusement.

Is it possible to hate someone you've only known for a few hours? No one had ever laughed at me the way he seemed determined to do. People scolded me for unruly behavior, or warned me about my pranks, or were occasionally amazed by my bravery and cleverness (yes, they were!), but no one of my acquaintance regarded me with such unholy amusement as this mysterious stranger.

"Never mind," I said. "Where have you been?"

"I was about to go riding, but remembered my gauntlets before getting halfway down the back stairs. Does that disappoint you, Miss Ryder?"

"Why would you ride at this hour? It's barely light."

"Odd," he muttered, a perplexed expression lifting one brow. "No one has ever before questioned my habits. If anyone ever had, I believe I should have told them that it was none of their business. But you, my dear Miss Ryder, I shall tell the true reason. I ride at this hour because I wish to ride at this hour. There!'' He said this as though it were a great concession to me.

"You should let someone know," I snapped, exasperated. "Otherwise there might not be anyone at the stables to help you, or one of the servants might think you were a thief wandering around the house in the dead of night."

"Now that I cannot believe." He made a sweeping gesture toward the back stairs. "I've heard more than one person moving about in this area during the night. And if any of them were thieves, I don't believe your footman captured them. Have you many valuables to attract thieves to Hastings?"

"I'm sure we have just as many valuables as the next family—heirlooms, jewelry, that sort of thing." My head came up sharply. "What do you mean, you've heard people on the stairs during the night?"

"I'm a light sleeper," he confessed. "My room is too close to the stairs for me to be ignorant of the passage of several sets of feet. No doubt it was the servants locking up or checking out the random noises in the night. Or perhaps your mother or sister are restless sleepers and made their way down to the kitchen for a glass of warm milk."

His eyes seemed to demand some answer to this last remark, but I was in no mood to satisfy his curiosity even though he had provoked my own. "Hmmm. I think perhaps we must switch your room, Sir John. It won't do to have your rest disturbed by the comings and goings of the household."

"No." His voice brooked no argument. "I don't wish to have my room changed, Miss Ryder. I can tolerate these, ah, small disturbances very nicely. And the room is so convenient for my early-morning rides."

Frustrated and feeling that no further purpose would be served by my remaining there, especially since his gaze wandered with interest over my dishabille, I put my chin up and said, "Have a pleasant ride, sir. No doubt I shall see you later in the day. I don't, as a rule, leave my bed this early."

"Too bad," he murmured as he let himself into his room.

·4·

You would have thought that anyone who used as an excuse the necessity of hunting out some carriage horses would have set about the task immediately. Not Sir John. He spent the whole day wandering about the house, making eyes at Amanda, and further investigating the grounds and stables. I could hardly bear not to chide him upon this matter, but Mama kept giving me a stern look, as though I might spoil Amanda's chances of landing such a catch.

Pooh! We didn't know a thing about the man. For all our knowledge from Robert, Sir John might be poor as a church mouse. Except for the excuse of looking for carriage horses. It would be easy enough for him to pretend he couldn't find what he needed. His clothes were no assurance of his having them ready, either; I've heard over and over again that young bloods in London buy their clothes on tick and forget to pay their tailors. An inexcusable habit, in my opinion. Tailors' families have to eat, too.

It was not until the second day after he arrived that Sir John mentioned his intention of visiting Overview Stables. These are on the Newmarket Road only a few miles from Hastings. When he brought up the subject at breakfast, Mama smiled kindly on him.

"An admirable place, Sir John," she said. "Robert likes their horses almost as much as those he's had from Hinchly Farms. But you should take your time, you know. Perhaps a picnic would make your search a little easier. Mrs. Cooper could pack you a nuncheon to be eaten by the river on your way, or on the way back.''

''What a delightful idea,'' Sir John exclaimed. ''I don't suppose you could spare your daughter to accompany me?''

He was looking at Amanda, of course. His curricle held only two riders, and the groom up behind. Mama would hardly allow Amanda to go out alone in his company, I thought with some satisfaction, nor would Amanda herself be persuaded that it was a proper thing to do.

''I believe I could spare her,'' Mama agreed with a coy look. ''Any plans we have for tatting or cutting flowers for the hall can easily be put off to another day.''

Amanda was blushing prettily. ''How kind of you to offer, Sir John. There is nothing I like better than a picnic, and I know just the spot for it.''

I could not believe my ears! Had their wits gone begging? It was one thing for either of us to go off with a neighborhood lad for a few hours, someone my mother had known for years, but this stranger! Surely they were mad. Not even Robert's introduction made it excusable.

''Amanda won't be of the least use to you in finding the way or in choosing your horses,'' I said. ''She has the worst sense of direction of anyone I know, and can't distinguish one road from another. And as for her knowledge of horses . . .'' I laughed merrily. ''You would be ashamed to be caught dead on any nag my sister chose. It would be broken-winded and forever throwing out splints, to say nothing of being the showiest nag you've ever laid eyes on. You had much better take me with you.''

The three of them stared at me. Mama managed to

kick me under the table, though I was sitting a considerable distance from her. Dutch moved at a surprising pace to get out of the way of Amanda's delicate little foot. Sir John was the first to recover, and the only one who didn't, presumably, try to kick me.

"Your thoughtfulness is much appreciated, Miss Ryder. I don't for a moment, however, expect my companion to offer me advice on choosing my carriage horses. Perhaps you will be so good as to give me your opinion once I've determined on a pair for your brother. As to my own choice . . ." He shrugged his broad shoulders. "I didn't even take my father's advice in such matters once I came of age."

"Of course you won't go with him," my mother declared indignantly as she recovered the spoon she had dropped. "It is Amanda whom he desires to accompany him. I'm sure she can give him adequate directions." She looked thoughtful for a brief moment and then added, "But perhaps it would be wisest for him to speak with one of our grooms before they leave."

"Isn't Jeremy Woods expected today?" I asked, playing my last card.

"I'm sure I don't know if Robert's old friend intends to call," Amanda muttered, tossing her napkin down on the table as she rose. "I can be ready in an hour, if that will suit you," she said to the baronet.

"Perfect." He rose to his feet with all the grace of a fencer, smiling so warmly on her that I thought her lips must catch fire. "I'll be sure not to overset the curricle with such a precious cargo, but you must wear a bonnet that will protect you a little from the wind. My horses would be disappointed if I didn't set them properly to their paces."

Sixteen-mile-an-hour ones, if I knew anything about it, which I certainly did. Amanda would have her heart in her throat the whole time. She can't abide driving fast and begs anyone who takes her out to keep the beasts to a walk. But I knew she would not dare come straight out with the request of Sir John. Perhaps after a few minutes she would say, "Why, I do believe we're going so fast that I cannot see the landscape quite as well as I would like." What a pest she is. No doubt Sir John would be like all the other men and reluctantly draw his horses in to a mild trot in an effort to please her. Humph.

I went to see them off, just to discomfit Amanda. Yes, yes, I know that was unpleasant of me, but there it is. She was standing in her finest bonnet, tied down with a length of Mama's best net, and pretending to admire Sir John's chestnuts. "How superbly matched they are," she cried, eyeing them with alarm.

"Huge," I said. "They are the largest beasts I've seen in many a month. I suppose they're extraordinarily fast?"

"As the wind," he agreed. "Miss Amanda will never have had such a drive before, I trust."

"Oh, you mustn't hurry them on my account," she insisted, her face paling.

"They're impatient unless they're doing a hearty pace. Don't worry your head about that."

I turned my back to him and grinned at her maliciously. "Oh, you'll have a splendid time. Flying along in that fragile curricle! How lucky you are, my dear sister."

She almost stamped her foot with anger at me, but recalled herself in time. "Of course I shall." And she lifted her round chin so high I thought her pink bonnet would fall off backward.

Sir John handed her into the curricle, and I could see what he meant by its balance. Just Amanda's weight made it tilt precariously. He positioned himself carefully as he set foot in it himself and gathered up the reins. Positioning himself carefully meant that he placed himself very close to my sister. I have to admit that he looked splendid sitting there, his gauntlets tightly gripping the leather straps, his boots braced against the footboard of the curricle. Those broad shoulders could not help but touch Amanda's, and his muscular thighs must have done the same, though I couldn't precisely see.

His artistry in setting the horses to their paces was something I could appreciate, and I suppose it must have been what drew Robert's notice to him in the first place. Robert is a great admirer of a true whipster. I wouldn't have been surprised to learn that Sir John was one of those wild blades who had actually driven a mail coach. Rumors of such things reached us even in the country, and the baronet seemed just the sort of fellow who wouldn't be able to resist that challenge.

When they had disappeared toward the Newmarket Road, I wandered back into the stable, feeling both neglected and disgruntled. Why did everyone assume that Amanda . . . Well, it didn't really matter to me, so I refused to think about it. When I had made my way to Lofty's box stall, I stood there running my fingers through her forelock and whispering sweet words in her flickering ears. Before long our groom, Jed, appeared at my side.

"I'm that surprised it weren't you went with the gentleman," he said, grinning up with his mouthful of missing teeth. "Weren't he goin' off to look at horses at Overview?"

"Yes, and he assures us that he doesn't need any help in choosing them."

Jed laughed. "Small wonder, ma'am. Never seen such prime 'uns as those chestnuts. Groom said he got 'em near Chelverton goin' on two years. Must be a breeder good as Hinchly, eh?"

"That's what I was thinking. But he'd never heard of Hinchly. Probably because the man's so irascible with strangers. We're the lucky ones, not having all his horses sent off to London. Do you suppose none of his horses has ever come up at Tattersall's?''

''Mayhap. Mr. Robert wouldn't let any of his end up there. Which minds me. That cousin of your'n be riding Thunder again, even one nighttime. Is that all right by you?''

''No, but I won't stop him.'' Another thought had occurred to me and I turned from Lofty to ask him. ''Did Sir John ride out early this morning? About dawn? Or perhaps earlier?''

There was a slight hesitation before he answered. ''Can't rightly say, miss. I weren't in the stables yet. A touch of the stomach. You could ask Cooper. He'd know for sure.''

How strange, I thought. Jed used to spend every waking moment at the stables, stomach upset or not. I'd even seen him more than once with terrible tooth-ache working away at the brasses. But the matter immediately disappeared from my mind when I went in search of Cooper. He's been in charge of our stables for as long as his wife has been our cook, and he's almost as attached to us young folks as she is, having put us on our first ponies.

I found him in the large tack room, repairing a saddle that had seen better days. The walls were hung with brasses and terrets, horseshoes and harness. When Cooper looked up I was struck for the first-time by how white his hair had become; he was getting old. His eyes were a bit rheumy but his fingers moved as nimbly as ever over the leather. When I asked him my question, he scratched his head.

''Well, now, seems everybody and his brother took an early ride. That Mr. Cummings was out before I came down, and then Sir John showed up before dawn was full broke.'' He frowned. ''And I'da sworn Antelope had been ridden, too, 'cept who was there to take her out but you?''

Antelope is my mother's favorite. Mr. Cummings, my Cousin Bret, rides Thunder, though no one really considers him a good-enough rider to be up on the magnificent mount. Robert would have taken the horse to town if we hadn't all known London was no place for such a restless animal. Thunder needed to be ridden regularly, and hard, in order to keep him in good shape and spirits. I wondered if Sir John would offer to take him over for the duration of his stay. It would be a treat to see Sir John up on that powerful beast.

''Well, I certainly didn't ride Antelope. I don't go out riding in the middle of the night.'' But he'd made me wonder. ''Why did you think she'd been ridden?''

''Oh, she'd been rubbed down, and all, but I know that little mare. She had the look of hard ride under her belt, if you take my meaning.''

I did. ''Didn't Jed say whether he'd rubbed her down?''

''He don't answer questions like that, miss. Not for me nor nobody.''

''But why? What has he to hide, for heaven's sake?''

''Begging your pardon, miss, but I wouldn't know. He's a law unto himself that one, and your ma won't hear of him being dismissed.''

''Well, I should think not,'' I replied, indignant. ''He's the best groom we've ever had. But I can't imagine why he wouldn't answer some simple questions.''

''Mayhap they ain't so simple,'' the old man muttered, patting the saddle with a kind of finality.

Seeing that I wasn't going to get any more out of him, I took myself off. There was entirely too much mystery suddenly cluttering up the place. Hastings is, usually, just an ordinary and uncomplicated spot, comfortable and rather dull, actually. For some reason, the prospect of a mystery didn't excite me as it might have. I could smell trouble. And trouble wasn't what we needed right then, since Robert was heir apparent to an earldom.

My father was the younger son of a younger son of a not-very-prolific family. By the unassuming way he lived, no one would have guessed he might become an earl during his lifetime. He was more interested in his books and crops than in the lineage of his family or the privileges the aristocracy could claim.

But Papa died before his great-uncle, which left Robert in line for the earldom.

The earl, Lord Stonebridge, is more than eighty years old and could pop off at any time. He's a very high stickler and would have produced an heir if he could. It galls him that not one of his three wives managed to provide a living heir. There were a few sickly babies, I believe, but none of them survived.

Lord Stonebridge likes to treat Robert as if he were some sort of medieval retainer, insisting that Robert drop everything and hurry off to Stonebridge Castle at the slightest hint from his highness. Stonebridge says Robert has a lot to learn before he'll be ready to accept the mantle of his aristocratic heritage. Robert laughs at this, of course. He can be whatever kind of person he wishes, whether he's a lord or not.

Anyhow, it wouldn't do to have something untoward happen at Hastings, because Lord Stonebridge has spies in the very gateposts. When one of our horses went missing for a few days, he heard about it and wrote to tell Mama that she was not handling matters properly. He said he knew just the man Robert should appoint to oversee the stables. Instead, I accepted the responsibility myself, and no one has had any cause to complain.

We would not pay Lord Stonebridge the slightest notice, except that he has a habit of writing letters to the newspapers, which almost always see fit to print what he has to say. Not because of the wisdom of the letters, I'm convinced, but because these letters invariably prove a great embarrassment to someone. Quite often us. No one at Hastings will forget the day the *Morning Post* arrived with a letter by the earl deriding the state of the countryside when a family in Cambridgeshire could mismanage their stables so badly that their horses simply strayed off for a day or two. It made us the laughingstock of the neighborhood.

So I'd rather things remained placid here until the old fellow meets his Maker, and his three previous wives.

I ran into Cousin Bret on my way back to the house. He hadn't made it down to breakfast—he seldom does before ten—and he'd obviously just heard that Amanda was off with Sir John for the day.

"How could your mother let her go off with a virtual stranger?" he demanded on seeing me. "We don't know the first thing about the fellow and he seems a bit of a loose screw to me. You won't credit it, but Hughes and I discovered him that first day hanging about the pond, as if he owned the place. Wouldn't even present his letter to us."

There's nothing I hate more than to be in agreement with Cousin Bret, so I pretended that I wasn't. "If he's a friend of Robert's, I'm sure he's perfectly harmless."

"Hah. You haven't the slightest idea what your brother gets up to in London."

"Do you?"

"No, but I'm sure he's no angel there. And this one," said he, giving his head a thrust in the direction of the departed curricle, "I'm sure I've heard his name and that his reputation is that of a rake and a gambler. Your mother shouldn't have allowed a delicate young

thing like Amanda to rush off with him, and only his
groom in attendance. His groom, you will note. Not
one of Hastings' grooms. Not that there aren't those
at Hastings who would be less than useless, either.''

I knew he wanted me to ask which, but I refused to
give him the satisfaction. ''They've only gone to Overview Stables, and to have a picnic on their return. No
harm will come to Amanda.''

''How can you possible know that?'' he sneered.
''She's the most trusting creature. And so easily influ-
enced.''

He said this with approbation, and I nearly laughed
at him. Amanda, trusting! Not a bit of it. And she's
about as impressionable as a major in the Horse
Guards. Except where Sir John was concerned. And
he wasn't going to make any headway with her.
Amanda has her principles. She would allow him no
liberties until they had stood together before a man of
the cloth. What was I thinking! She was not going to
marry Sir John. Not if I had anything to say to it!

''Amanda has more sense than you credit her with,''
I said.

His sneer deepened until his nostrils flared. ''You
are so naïve, Cousin Catherine.''

He turned away from me and stalked off, which was
perfectly all right with me.

Sir John and my sister didn't return for hours. I sat
in the arbor, waiting for them. Not that I intended to
spy on them; I was waiting for the return of the picnic
basket. I had learned at our cold nuncheon that Mrs.
Cooper sent the last of her raspberry tarts for their
picnic. No one makes better raspberry tarts than Mrs.
Cooper, and I'd been anticipating another since they
disappeared from the dining room the previous evening.

What could be keeping them all that time? It would

have taken Sir John no more than a few hours to drive and learn the history of every horse at Overview Stables.

So their picnic, near the river, under a stand of larch trees—as I learned later—had lasted for several hours as well. And what had they done during all that time? Surely no more than talked to each other. Perhaps Amanda had flirted with him a little, lying on the ground on the rug I'd seen peeking out from under the curricle's seat. She would have blinked up at him and smiled, her loveliest, shyest smile. Several of the neighborhood boys were captivated by that smile.

And what would he have done, that rake in gentleman's clothing? He would have regarded her with those expressive eyes, all admiration and appreciation of her beauty. Certainly not of her wit! She would have told him about how she spent her days, netting purses and helping Mama plan the menus and overseeing the church's charitable activities. She might have told him about how remarkable her old horse Daisy was. If Sir John had seen it, he would know just how deplorable the old nag had become, but he would be wise enough not to mention it. Amanda would also, no doubt, tell a few tales about me. She can no more resist telling tales about me than I can resist taunting her.

Anyhow. They arrived home all smiles, and with everything in the picnic basket totally devoured. Not even a few polite crumbs to assure Mrs. Cooper that there had been more than enough for them to eat. Sir John alone could not be blamed, for although Amanda's appetite wasn't all that hearty, she adored cream buns and the aforementioned raspberry tarts.

They stopped to speak with me on their way into the house. Amanda's eyes widened with surprise. "What in heaven's name are you doing here?" she asked. "I expected you to be out on Lofty pounding through the countryside on such a day."

That was just to prove to him, no doubt, that I'm the greatest hoyden in nature and would scarcely be caught dead swinging on the lattice seat in the arbor like an ordinary girl. "I was waiting to see if you brought back any raspberry tarts," I replied.

"Nary a one," Sir John assured me cheerfully. "I think I must have eaten three of them myself, and your sister . . ."

"Yes, yes, I believe we did finish all of them." She gave him a coy, scolding look as she spoke. "I'll not be called to task for eating a few raspberry tarts."

"No one would dare call you to task for anything," he assured her. Really, it was quite sickening, the sweet looks they gave each other. What the devil had gotten into Amanda, anyhow? Couldn't she see what he was? Why, if she knew about him at the pond, or how he'd spoken to me that very morning, she would blush deep as a beet and likely never speak to him again. Our vicar had convinced her that the righteous never associate with the devil, lest they become infected with evil. He has a way with words, our vicar.

Amanda waved her fingers at us and continued on toward the house, but Sir John sat down across from me on the other swing. When she was out of sight, he said, "She's the most agreeable young woman I've met in years. So unspoiled!"

"And I suppose you have every intention of spoiling her," I snapped, plagued by the knowing look in his eyes. "Well, you'll catch cold at that, my dear sir. She's something of a prude, and certainly not anyone to tolerate the slightest indiscreet move on your part."

"I'm well aware of it."

"Ha! You've done nothing but make up to her since you arrived."

"I'm well aware of that, too."

I refused to be drawn by him, since I was convinced he meant only to tease me. It might have been a good time to ask him what he was up to, but I couldn't bring myself to do it. Certainly he wouldn't have answered me honestly. With a shake of my riding costume's skirts I jumped up and glared at him. "I'm off for a ride, then. Don't bother to see me to the stables. You will want to change and spend some time with Mama, making yourself agreeable to her."

"Yes," he agreed as he rose. "That's precisely what I intend to do."

"Robert has obviously fallen into bad company." I turned to leave him, only to feel his hand on my arm. Surprised—nay, shocked—my eyes flew up to his. He considered me for a long, intent moment while his hand remained warm on my flesh. A rueful smile formed at the corner of his wide mouth.

"Later," he murmured.

"Humph!" I retorted, and stalked off.

·5·

That evening at dinner it seemed to me that there was nothing so smug as Sir John, with Mama smiling warmly at him and Amanda hanging on his every word. I did not lend myself to this oozy scene. Amid their gaiety, I was solemn, busy with my own thoughts. If he chose to believe I was bored with his conversation, so much the better.

After dinner we played at cards until the tea tray was brought in. Mama and I were winning, but it only seemed to agitate her. Usually she found a hand at whist relaxing, though I could remember several occasions on which this wasn't true, especially right after my father died. She would be gazing at her cards when suddenly her head would snap up and she would stare straight at the fireplace, or at a panel on the wall or a window covering. And she would mutter to herself.

Well, let me be entirely truthful. When she muttered, it was not to herself. This is a rather difficult thing to admit, but my mother talked to ghosts. And not just since my father died, actually. There had been earlier occasions when I had come upon her in some dark reach of the house, earnestly speaking to . . . a blank wall.

My mother was not mad. She had simply developed a rather unique conception of religion. Her inspiration came from our country church, by way of her own idea of the hereafter. She believed that we were all surrounded by the dear departed all the time and that you could speak to them and they would hear you.

We have all done it, in a way. Consider: you are in the sitting room doing a little repair work on a bonnet whose ribbon has become frayed. If your mind happens to wander off to your dead Aunt Sophy, you might, if you are so inclined, think something like, Dear Aunt Sophy, I do miss you. Those plum cakes you used to make were so exquisite, and you were always so kind to remember me on my birthday. In Mama's case, she simply said these things aloud.

When he was alive, my father made it quite clear to Mama that she must curb this kind of behavior when other people were around. Mama herself didn't understand this; it seemed the most natural thing in the world to talk with ghosts. However, Papa was the one person in the world she really wanted to please, and she ordinarily behaved acceptably. She had not, for instance, embarrassed us before Cousin Bret.

Her little quirk only became problematic, really, after Papa died and she took to believing that he spoke to her. Now I was alarmed to see her slip into an absent reverie right in front of Sir John. I gave her a nudge under the table, and I saw Amanda grab hold of her wrist.

Sir John pretended that nothing out of the ordinary was happening. It was his turn to play a card, and he went straight ahead and tossed it onto the table, assuming, I suppose, that such a movement would draw Mama out of her unnatural preoccupation.

Nothing of the sort!

"Yes, Harold, I am well aware of it," she said, still staring at the empty grate. Harold was my father's name.

"Mama, it's your turn," Amanda whispered urgently, poking Mama in her side.

But Mama was not to be deterred from her little conversation. "He seems a nice lad, and obviously well-enough-to-do," she explained to my father. No one around her doubted that she was speaking of Sir John; Amanda flushed an alarming shade of crimson. "Well, of course Robert has not always had the best judgment in his friendships, but I'm sure this time is different."

"Would you like another cup of tea?" I asked the baronet. Amanda was speechless. Making a great rattle with the cups and saucers was no trouble for me, but it failed to rouse Mama from her trance.

"I believe I will," the baronet said.

"A splendid idea," Amanda gushed, recovering herself. "That was milk and two sugars, was it not?"

He agreed that it was, but he never took his eyes from Mama. She had ceased talking and was listening with an earnest countenance, occasionally nodding or frowning. After some time, she said, "Oh, don't leave," and then looked crestfallen. Her attention never did return to us, though. As if the hand were finished, she pushed her cards toward the center of the table and rose.

"A lovely game. We must certainly play again. If you will excuse me, Sir John, I'm a trifle fatigued. The girls will entertain you." She walked off in a daze, rubbing one hand softly against her brow.

Sir John was on his feet, a polite expression on his face. No one said anything after the door closed behind her. Amanda looked as though she wished to hide under the nearest chair. After a moment I cleared my throat and said stoutly, "You must forgive Mama's inattention. Ever since Papa died, she has been a little distracted."

"Oh, yes, indeed," Amanda agreed. "Poor lamb. She was so exceedingly devoted to him that it has 'distracted' her a little, as Catherine says."

Sir John resumed his seat and gathered up his cards. Without a word he shuffled the deck and glanced kindly at each of us. "Shall the three of us have a hand at loo?"

Which was the essence of good manners, I supposed, but I knew he was storing it all up in his mind. For whatever purpose. Who would not?

Sir John said good night to my sister very prettily, taking her hand between both of his and lifting it to his lips. I could have sworn that he winked at me when he was kissing her plump little fist, though, which served to confuse me more than ever. One thing I did decide was that he was trying to hoodwink us all in some way or other, and I determined to keep a vigil again that night, especially since I was certain he had gone out the night before, when I'd been too exhausted to do more than fall into my bed.

My method of spying was simply to place myself right around the corner from his room. I dragged a covering from my bed and made myself as comfortable as possible, wishing that I dared to light a candle and read for the duration. Fortunately, the floor is not comfortable, and I knew I would rouse easily with the slightest sound. To be ready for immediate action, I wore my riding clothes, hoping that I would not be called upon to saddle Lofty myself, as I was not particularly quick about it and had never done it in the dark.

The first several hours of my vigil were spent in fitful sleep. Around two in the morning I was awakened by a sound in the hall, but it came from another direction entirely. Both Mama's and Cousin Bret's rooms were in the facing wing and it could have been either of them, needing to use the water closet in the night. Just as I was about to drift off to sleep again I heard the door at the head of the stairs creak. I leapt to my feet and poked my head around the corner to see who it was.

Too late. The door was already closing behind the midnight adventurer. I had to make a quick decision about what to do, and I decided to see whether Sir John was still in his room. Since the only view I had through the keyhole was a black emptiness, I tried the door. He hadn't locked it and, with great caution, I turned the handle, inching it around until I could feel it would swing clear. Even though I got a wider perspective on the room, I couldn't tell if the baronet was in his bed. My eyes had adjusted to the dark, but there seemed to be mounds of bedclothes in the four-poster. With the curtains draped along the sides, it was impossible to be sure if there was a body in the bed or not.

Did I dare walk across the floor to his bed to check? My courage nearly failed me. What if he was there and awake? I had made almost no sound opening the door, but he might be suffering from sleeplessness, or be an extraordinarily light sleeper. Hadn't he mentioned being able to distinguish all sorts of noises in the hall on his first night? I braced myself and moved silently across the cold floorboards and the Axminster carpet in my bare feet. I made not the slightest whisper of sound.

And yet when I came close enough to see if he was in the bed, a hand of gripping strength caught my arm, pulling swiftly downward so that I was forced to my knees. A whimper escaped me and I found my arm abruptly released.

"So it's you again," he grumbled. "What did you have in mind this time, my dear?"

"My arm is going to be bruised. You couldn't possibly just ask who was there, could you? I shall have marks on my arm for a week." My mutterings were more hysteria than anger. He had frightened me by his abrupt and decisive movement.

"How was I to know it was you?" he retorted. "It might have been an assassin, ready to plunge a knife into my heart as I slept."

"Dear heaven, what outlandish novel were you reading when you fell asleep?" I demanded. "We don't have assassins here at Hastings. Not one of our visitors has ever had a knife plunged into his heart as he slept."

"What are you doing here, Catherine?"

His voice had softened and I could see his eyes glitter in the darkness. His hand had already returned to rub my wrist, and now it tightened slightly, drawing me toward his bed. I was still on my knees, and this movement brought my face alarmingly close to his. I could feel the warm breath from his lips as he spoke.

"You have the oddest habit of wandering around in the night. Do you take after your mother in that respect?"

"My mother does not wander around in the middle of the night," I said.

"No? My mistake. Well, if it is not a family habit, please explain what you're doing here."

"I was merely checking to see that you were in your room. When I heard a noise on the stairs, I thought it might be you going out."

"How in heaven's name did you hear anything on the stairs? Your room is far too distant for you to hear anything but an avalanche on the stairs."

Since I had no intention of telling him where I had been sleeping, I freed myself from his clasp with a swift jerk of my hand and leapt to my feet. "I'm going back to bed."

"Catherine, Catherine. Don't be so hasty. We might have a little interesting conversation, you and I."

Suspecting him of being a rake, I had no doubt that

this phrase was a euphemism for something wholly indecent. My fingers itched to slap him, but his hand shot out and grabbed my wrist again.

"Now, now. You misunderstand me, my dear child. I meant only that you and I should talk. There is something conducive to sharing confidences in the dead of night, where not a single candle burns nor a ray of light pierces the draperies." His voice was like silk and I felt myself swallow hard. "I was not suggesting something improper. Your brother is a great friend of mine, remember. That is not a friendship I would jeopardize for the kind of accommodation I can so easily find elsewhere."

I drew back sharply from him, though he still retained his hold on my wrist. "I knew you were a rake! From the moment I laid eyes on you, I knew you were the most outrageous creature."

He laughed. "And from the moment I laid eyes on you, my fair one, I knew you had the kind of fiery spirit that would warm me a little too much for my own good." He had raised himself up on one elbow. It was plain to me that he had no nightshirt on, and I trembled slightly. "I have no intention of ravishing you, though I don't say you are wrong about my reputation."

"Amanda could not be brought to speak so much as a word to you if she knew you were anything of the sort."

A brief, strange smile gave way to a mock-serious frown. "I know. You won't divulge my secret, will you? Just at this point in our acquaintance, I fear Miss Amanda would not believe you. It would make you look too much like a spoilsport, since there is no way you could offer proof of such a thing."

He was perfectly right, though it galled me to admit it. "I'm sure in time you will demonstrate it admirably without my help,'' I said huffily. ''Please release my arm.''

''Certainly.'' Though he loosened his fingers, he did not actually let go of my hand. Instead, he drew it to his lips and kissed the tender skin on the inside of my wrist. A slight suction there caused a most astonishing sensation in the pit of my stomach. I had every intention of pulling my hand away from him, then, but he continued to kiss it, the tips of my fingers, and the back of my hand until I seemed to tingle all over.

Somehow it would have felt rude of me to withdraw it just at that point. With his head bent down and the thick brown hair so close that I could have touched it with my lips, I found myself frozen. When he withdrew and beckoned me to lower my head, I shook it fiercely and backed away from him. With a sigh of regret, he released my hand. I fled from the room. Well, what could I possibly have said to him at a time like that?

Afraid that he would follow me, I hastily gathered my covers from the floor and lumped them in my arms. I raced for my room and closed the door with a decided thump, leaning against it and breathing so hard you would have thought I'd run all the way up the peak behind Hastings in a minute flat. What was he thinking of to behave that way with me in the middle of the night? Or any other time, for that matter? Had he kissed Amanda's hand like that?

There was something alarming about this man. First thing in the morning I planned to write Robert, asking hard questions about Sir John. If he was a rogue, I wanted to know. Being a rake was another matter entirely. A man of his age and looks and prospects was rather expected to be a bit of a hand with the ladies, but if he treated them dishonorably, that was something different. I only hoped my brother would be open with me about what was going on. As I climbed into bed, I decided to post my letter in town—much safer than having it lie about on the salver in the hall where someone might see and remove it.

I closed my eyes and the next thing I knew it was late in the morning, with the sun streaming through my window. Late, in our household, is about ten o'clock. I would have missed breakfast entirely, except that Mama was forced to leave the food out longer on account of Cousin Bret never appearing before that hour. Which meant that I would be forced to share my meal with him. If I hadn't been so hungry, I would have skipped my breakfast entirely.

Sure enough, he was seated there in all his sartorial splendor. He had never understood the concept of dressing informally in the country. My cousin rose graciously to his feet and regarded me with a sardonic curl of his fleshy lips. "You're a trifle late this morning, aren't you, cousin?"

I allowed him to hold my chair for me. "No later than you."

"I suppose the rest of them have already eaten and gone about their business. I had hoped to catch a glimpse of Cousin Amanda this morning. I thought she looked peaked at dinner last night."

"I assure you she is quite in bloom. You needn't concern yourself with her health."

"I always concern myself with her health. She's a delicate young woman."

"Balderdash! She's no more delicate than I." When I could see that he meant to retort, I forestalled him by saying, "Her robustness is apparent to everyone but you, Cousin Bret. You are determined upon her delicacy only because she doesn't like horses and refuses to ride them now that her precious Daisy has been turned out to grass."

"She should bring herself to be more comfortable with horses," he said.

This from the man who thought he was a genius with horses. Who thought he could control Robert's horse, Thunder. Once when Cousin Bret dismounted—he told us he dismounted, but I have a grave suspicion that he was actually thrown—Thunder took off for the stable and Cousin Bret was left to walk the five miles home.

He had continued to make his pronouncements on Amanda's peculiar habits regarding horses. "It's strange, with all the rest of you absolutely mad for them, that she has taken this aversion. No doubt it is an affectation that will disappear under the blandishments of one dear to her."

I snorted at this obviously ludicrous suggestion. "She isn't going to change her mind about horses."

"But she drove out with Sir John yesterday."

"More of a tribute to Sir John than a change of heart."

Cousin Bret eyed me reproachfully. "You're quite mistaken. Sir John is not the sort of man who would appeal to your sister. Cousin Amanda needs someone with stability of character and definition of purpose."

I refused to discuss the matter further with him. He's as stubborn as a man comes, and he was welcome to believe what he wished, so long as it didn't interfere with my plans. "Where have you been the last few evenings?" I inquired, to change the subject and because I was curious.

His countenance changed abruptly. "Nowhere special. I've gone into Cambridge to visit friends. The Mortons. A superior couple whom I've known since the days I spent in London. Most intelligent and worthy. They would be an excellent addition to your acquaintance, Cousin Catherine. Their example would be a good influence."

"I do hate being insulted at breakfast," I informed him as I buttered a roll.

"No insult was intended, I assure you. It is a matter of polish. Mrs. Morton could advise you how to go on, as she has spent considerable time in London among the *ton*. As I recall, your Season in London was something of a disaster." I frowned, but he ignored me, patting his full lips with a linen napkin. "Your sister would have made more use of a Season to acquire the necessary town bronze. She's so amenable to instruction."

Which I am not, of course. I could scarcely bear to remain in the same room with him. But there was something he'd said that nagged at me. Not all the stupid talk of polish, but about the Mortons. Could he possibly have visited them two nights in a row? Most unlikely. And hadn't Jed said something about Thunder being taken out only one evening?

"Where do the Mortons live?" I asked.

"On Trumpington Street."

"Did they have some special entertainment, to draw you there two nights in a row?"

He had been chewing on a sausage but his eyes swung alertly to me. "What's that you're asking? Two nights in a row?"

"Isn't that what you meant? That you had been there both last night and the night before?"

For a fraction of a second he hesitated, and then he speared another bite with his fork. "Yes, I was there both nights. We began discussing a new book David had received, and wished to continue our talk, with some reading *en famille*, on the following evening."

"I see." Nothing in his expression encouraged me to believe him. From the time he was a small boy it has been easy enough to tell when my cousin was lying, though he never once would admit it. Lying was actually one of his few endearing qualities, I always thought. I mean, at least it indicated a little imagina-

tion. Otherwise, one would have been forced to con-
clude that he possessed none at all.

Unfortunately, Cousin Bret usually lied to keep himself out of trouble. I couldn't fathom his reasons for
doing it now, but I had every intention of finding them
out.

·6·

My sister spent most of her spare moments with Sir John, but her spare moments weren't as many as she might have liked. I insisted that she not neglect her standard duties, such as arranging meals with Mrs. Cooper, and overseeing the mending of the linens, and cutting the flowers for the table, and making sure that the underhousemaids used the proper mixture of soap lees, turpentine, and pipeclay to clean the marble.

Oh, we neither of us were such ladies of leisure as some city folk might imagine. Mama insisted that we learn every fine point of being in charge of a domestic staff and running a large, and possibly not wholly rich, household. Why, when we were younger, she even saw to it that we learned to make cheeses and hang the meats to cure.

Amanda was embarrassed by this sort of task. She was much more comfortable with an embroidery needle than a curd breaker. Not for the world would she have had Sir John see her go into the dairy. I had no such qualms. Coming on the said gentleman the next afternoon, and perhaps a bit disoriented by my memories of our last encounter, I chided him for walking into the house in muddy boots.

"Now where did you learn such despicable habits, Sir John?" I demanded. "Surely your mama would not have appreciated your dirt any more than we do.

Amanda will have to see that the housemaid takes special care with this floor now. I wouldn't be at all surprised if Amanda got down on her hands and knees and did it herself, just to make sure there's not a trace left by the next time you pass this way.''

Unfortunately, Amanda was just at that moment coming through the door from the kitchen, where she had undoubtedly been discharging some onerous duty, and she was furious with me. The color rose attractively in her cheeks and her eyes flashed with indignation. ''Catherine! How can you let your tongue run away with such lies? You may be sure that Mama will hear of this.''

Turning to Sir John, she hurriedly added, ''You must not heed a word she says. Of course you shall come into the hall in muddy boots if you wish. What on earth do we have housemaids for if not to clean up after us?''

Sir John looked down at his boots for the first time and seemed chagrined to find that they were, indeed, quite muddy. Though how they could have gotten that way, on this sunny day, I was at a loss to imagine. ''I heartily apologize,'' he said, offering his most charming smile to Amanda. ''If I had known my boots were muddy, I would have left them outside the back door.'' He made a move to remove them right then and there, but Amanda fluttered an agitated hand at him and begged him—yes, begged him—not to put himself to so much trouble.

''For I'm sure the worst of it is off now, and you won't leave a trail on your way to your room.'' She nervously pleated a handkerchief between her long, plump fingers.

''Or we might walk out in the garden until your boots dry, if you wished to come with me, and if your boots are not unbearably uncomfortable,'' I suggested with just a note of sarcasm in my voice.

Sir John raised a quizzical brow. "Perhaps Miss Amanda would accompany me. We wouldn't think of keeping you from your own duties," he added, smooth as glass. "I daresay you have the stables as your special province?"

He meant this as a set-down to me, but I'm proud of my supervision of the stables. His own horses were served well there, as even his groom would tell him. "The stables are indeed under my direction while my brother is away, Sir John. Which reminds me. Isn't it time for you to visit Hinchly Farms to see what they have to offer in the way of carriage horses? I could make myself available to go with you tomorrow. You'll need me to introduce you to old Hinchly. He's not the least bit tolerant of strangers. Perhaps Robert mentioned that to you?"

Rather than answer me, Sir John cast a questioning look at my sister. She shrugged and nodded. Not even Amanda could deny that it would be useful for him to have me along when he went to Hinchly Farms. "Very well." There was an absence of enthusiasm in his voice, which made me wonder if I'd imagined last night. "We'll go tomorrow. Early, if you please. So that we can be home in time for our midday meal."

No picnic for me! Well, he might be just the tiniest bit surprised by how I meant to handle the matter. Though I could see no reason to tell him in advance of my plans. "Early it is," I agreed cheerfully. "I can be ready by nine."

For a moment I thought he would quibble, but he made a fatalistic gesture. And grinned ruefully at my sister, so much as to say, "I don't wish to be away from you for a minute, but I will accomodate Miss Ryder if I must."

I felt there was no chance he would wander around that night, because he had to be up at a reasonable hour. He would want to breakfast and perhaps take his mount out for a quick ride before we left. It may have been lax of me, but I allowed myself a good night's sleep, something that was becoming a bit of a rarity for me since he'd arrived. It would do my complexion a world of good.

We met in the breakfast room, where he was eating a meal that would have done a starving man proud. Though he rose and waited for me to seat myself, I cannot say that he looked overpleased about our venture.

Sir John surprised me by saying, "Tell me about your cousin, Bretford Cummings. Why is it he doesn't stay in to enjoy the family's company most nights? It seems a trifle rude."

"Cousin Bret considers himself so much a member of our family that he prides himself on his ease in coming and going. Which is not the same as running tame here, you understand. He feels that he belongs here to the extent that he should be regarded with the same indulgence as my brother."

"Does he, now?" Sir John pursed his lips in something like annoyance. "What gives him that kind of privilege? Is he interested in marrying one of you?"

This was blunt talking. But I could be just as blunt. "He thinks to marry Amanda, but he is wide of the mark." Even I would not undercut Amanda by pretending that she liked Cousin Bret. No man of intelligence would believe something so ludicrous. "Amanda thinks he's a great coxcomb and a dead bore. In fact, we can't think why he comes to visit at all. When he was a child it was a matter of family honor with my father to have him visit, as it gave the cousins a chance to know one another. But it has been many years since anyone on this side has gotten any pleasure from the contact."

He ate another roll and an egg before continuing his observations. "He seems to have something of a penchant for riding off on one of your horses. Thunder, I believe his name is. Yet the stable lads are convinced he's not a good-enough rider to manage the beast.''

I sighed. "I suppose I could ban him from Thunder. He's going to ruin the horse's mouth, if he doesn't get himself thrown and killed. Robert was wonderful on Thunder, but he's not an easy horse to ride.''

"Don't you ride him, then?" Sir John asked, amused. "I thought you were the expert on horses.''

"I don't ride horses I cannot manage. You don't have to kill yourself to be able to judge the quality of an animal, you know.''

"Yes, I do know. I'm surprised you do." He eyed me with a bit more respect. But he didn't say anything except, "If you'll excuse me, I'll go out to the stables and see that the curricle is made ready. Why don't you join me there?''

Which was all to the good, because I had every intention of picking up the picnic basket in the kitchen and hauling it out there myself, before he could object. He couldn't easily refuse in front of the servants.

Mrs. Cooper had been delighted to be of service to me. When I came to fetch the basket, she lifted the cloth and pointed to a good bottle of wine. "Sir John is obviously a connoisseur. I won't try to pass off the everyday wine with him, but don't you go swilling the stuff down like it was lemonade, my girl. This is as powerful as it comes, and you'd do well to cultivate your palate by sipping it slowly and learning just how good it is.''

Mrs. Cooper has always been good at giving me reasons for doing things she wanted me to do. I think she picked the habit up from my mother, who always knew how to deal with me. My father was forever laying down laws that I chose to ignore because they seemed to have little rhyme or reason. Mrs. Cooper's suggestion that I develop my palate seemed eminently sensible. Mama hadn't the least interest in spirits, except the kind that talked to her. Mrs. Cooper added a corkscrew and a stock of horseradish to the basket before I left.

In the stableyard I found Sir John talking with Jed as the boy adjusted the neck collar on one of the chestnuts. When the baronet looked up and saw me with my basket, a dark scowl descended on his brow. "Hinchly Farms is farther away than Overview," I explained. "We'll need sustenance before we head back, and I know just the spot where we can stop."

"I was under the illusion we planned to return here for luncheon," he muttered as he took the basket from my hands.

"We can't expect Hinchly to offer us so much as a sip of water, and checking out carriage horses is thirsty work. Mrs. Cooper put in a good bottle of wine."

He twitched back the cloth. "Well, that's some comfort. Not that I don't appreciate small beer, but it's nice to have some variety."

After handing me up into the curricle, he went around to the other side and made some pretense of speaking to Jed. I could see his real purpose was to pretend that he had forgotten the picnic basket where he had set it down on the path, but I was not about to let him get away with that, no matter how unflattering his attempt. His own groom, Bill, eyed the basket doubtfully, and I said to him, "You'd best put it in now, or we'll forget it."

Sir John watched in silence as his groom did my bidding. I tucked the basket neatly under the seat to keep it out of the sun. The baronet climbed into his place beside me and I felt the carriage shift perilously. "I told you it was carefully balanced," he reminded me. "The slightest thing could overset it, so mind you don't get excited and jump about."

As if I would! "I'll remember." And I glared at him.

He gave his horses the office to start and they moved off at a pace so swift and smooth that I wondered Amanda had been able to tolerate it. We've had great carriage horses but none to match this pair. I would have given anything to have my hands on the reins, but I decided I'd have to bide my time before I asked that particular favor.

The narrowness of the seat and the precarious balance of the curricle made it necessary for Sir John to sit right up against me. I could feel the solidity of his thighs and the strength in his arms as he exerted pressure on the reins to guide his pair through the gate and left onto the lane leading to the Newmarket Road. His strength rather captivated me.

And I wasn't one to be lightly captivated by that sort of thing. I've driven out with any number of the local boys—they think of themselves as men—and I had yet to experience this particular sensation of awe. It might have been his hat tilted at a rakish angle, or the power in his forearms, or even the speed at which we drove. In any case, I was feeling decidedly in charity with him.

"We'll want to turn onto the Newmarket Road and travel on it for almost an hour," I said.

He nodded, then turned his head to say, "Your brother once told me you had a remarkable Season in London. I should like to know how many well-placed gentlemen you put to the blush."

"I did no such thing! My parents were there with me, and you may be sure that my behavior was as decorous as the next young lady's."

"Hmmm. Robert mentioned that you once had Lord Findlay positively in a rage after he had spent but an hour driving with you."

"Lord Findlay! The fellow is an odious beast. He

would not let me touch the reins, though his nags were nothing to brag about. And then he had the temerity to ask me to marry him. Marry him—when I had seen how he treated his horses! Well, who would not put a bee in such a one's curly beaver?'' I sniffed self-righteously. ''Where were you that spring? I'm sure I would have remembered if you had been in London then.''

''That was the spring my father had a serious bout with his heart. We thought he was recovering when he suddenly died.''

I murmured my sympathy.

Sir John was frowning off into the distance. ''I was several months in the country. It must have been midsummer by the time I returned to town. And, by God,'' he said, switching his incredulous gaze to my face, ''they were still talking about you.''

''Nonsense. No one noticed me at all.'' That was not precisely true, but the thought of all those people gossiping about me nearly put me to the blush.

But Sir John hadn't heard me. He was obviously trying to piece the story together for himself. ''I was the only one in town who hadn't been there to witness your assault on the capital. Poor Robert. No wonder he took to me, the only one who couldn't remind him of your escapades.''

I turned away so he wouldn't see the quick tears that pricked at my eyes. How unkind of him to revive that disastrous Season.

The good baronet was as oblivious to my distress as he could be. ''What an opportunity you give me, Miss Ryder, to hear the stories from the other side,'' said Sir John. ''Perhaps you would tell me how Augustus Thornside came to overturn his phaeton immediately after he'd left you off in Grosvenor Street.''

Being reminded of my time in London was the last thing I could have wished for. Everything had seemed to get out of hand so very quickly once we arrived there. I had expected London to be a place of delight, overflowing with excitement and diversions one could scarcely picture in the country. In fact, the atmosphere was stifling, every girl was expected to behave precisely as every other girl. And all those sharp-eyed mothers watching for a chance to guide their chicks toward the showy roosters. Ugh! It was not for me at all.

Sir John had not given up. "Or tell me what happened to William Carstairs? They say he's never been the same since you agreed to ride in Hyde Park with him on a particularly drizzly morning."

It was William Carstairs' mother who had made things so unpleasant. She had been a girl during my mother's Season, and she made it her task to let everyone in London know about the events that had happened then. And before long people were comparing me with her. Whenever I did anything out of the ordinary, such as speak before someone had spoken to me, they would shake their heads and say knowingly, "It's Penelope's daughter, you know. What else can you expect?"

Wisely, my mother ignored these comments, and I wouldn't for the life of me have asked her what they meant, but I became anxious to know, nonetheless. Apparently Robert was in more of a position to hear such tales than I was. And they say women gossip! He had the story from more than one source, and the most wicked version of it was from the Earl of Stonebridge, naturally.

No wonder Mama had been agitated as we prepared to travel down to London for the Season. She knew that the old tales would not be forgotten. How very brave of her to have managed to force herself to face those awful accusers.

My companion had finally noticed that I wasn't saying anything. "I should think you would wish to speak of your triumph after setting London on its ear," he teased me.

It was too much. "I did no such thing. I was merely the object of everyone's attention. They expected something terrible of me from the start."

"But why?" Sir John looked genuinely curious and I felt sure Robert had not told him the whole truth. Had Sir John not heard the rumors about Mama? If he hadn't, surely he should have been more surprised by her eccentricity the other night when she talked to a ghost? I felt it necessary to set him straight on a few things, for Mama's sake and my own.

"From the first moment we arrived in London it was apparent something was wrong. I kept catching whispers about my mother's Season, accompanied by half-concealed smiles or frowns of disapproval." Instinctively I raised my chin and took a firm grip on the seat. "I don't know how she bore it."

"Your mother strikes me as a woman who would scarcely notice such talk," he suggested kindly.

"Oh, she could bear it for herself with relative ease. But how could she bear it for her daughter? She apologized to me. Imagine!" I dashed away a stray tear and continued with all the fierceness that still raged in me. "My mother apologized to me for making my Season so miserable. It was not Mama who made my Season miserable, but all those people who insisted on having their fun pretending that Mama had done something reprehensible."

Sir John drew the horses in slightly, so that he could pay more attention to what I was saying. "Do you want to tell me what it was that they said? Being out of town at the time, I didn't hear anything of this. Only if you wish. I wouldn't want you to think I was satisfying some unnecessary curiosity."

The injustice of it all burned in me still and he was

a surprisingly sympathetic listener, with his head cocked to me even as he kept an eye on the chestnuts. "Mama had only an aging aunt to see her through her London Season, to provide her with the necessary information about customs and manners. She was sadly out of date, and there wasn't much money. Considerably less than most girls have for their stays in town. She had to be especially careful with her clothing allowance. They could only hire a chaise for the most important occasions. Mama learned to improvise with her bonnets and slippers, but one couldn't wear the same dress more than twice or people laughed at you."

"I can imagine." Sir John laid a comforting hand on my arm and I shivered.

"But she's such a clever woman," I exclaimed, to disguise my reaction from him. "Within a week she had spotted two other girls with insufficient funds and she had joined them in a very small conspiracy." He lifted a questioning brow and I had to laugh at the sheer audacity of my mama's plan. "They exchanged gowns! Truly. Mama was a remarkable seamstress even then and she was able to alter sizes and change the adornments so that no one would suspect the same gown had already been worn by another girl. It was marvelously inventive."

"Very ingenious. I suppose there are those who would have disapproved. But surely that wasn't enough to get her into real trouble."

"She couldn't just do it out in the open, you understand. When she had broached just the smallest detail to her aunt, the old lady was horrified, so Mama decided she must carry out her scheme in secret. And doing it in secret led to some rather strange adventures."

"Such as?"

I found myself gripping the seat again, with the wind cool on my flushed face. "She would get up before dawn and wrap the gowns carefully in a blanket to spirit them to one of the other girl's houses. None of the others was able to summon up such courage, I suppose. Though one or two of them could help with the sewing, Mama was always the delivery person. Mama was wonderfully spirited and unusually fearless for her age, I hear. It didn't bother her in the least to be out in London when dawn was breaking and there were no others abroad except farmers bringing their vegetables to Covent Garden and brewers delivering their ale to the public houses."

"Did she go alone?"

"She took her maid, a girl she'd known all her life, who thought nothing of their escapade. They were quick about their appointed rounds, always returning before the household was up."

"So how were they found out?"

"One morning, when they were on their way back from Upper Brook Street to Mount Row, they were waylaid by a band of reveling gentlemen who were just then returning home from their night's excesses. I don't suppose the men meant any real harm, but they were teasing my mother and the maid, insinuating that they were ladies of ill repute. Young blades, I understand, are likely to do that." I gave him a stern look.

"I've never accosted a woman in the street in my life, no matter how bosky I was," he protested.

I sniffed. "These fellows were not so high-minded. When one of them grabbed for the maid, to put his arm around her, she gave him a great crack on the skull with her only weapon, a knotty walking stick. And Mama was forced to fend off another with a few well-placed kicks . . ."

Sir John was laughing by this time. I heard the merry sound with a most welcome relief. "How wonderful!" he crowed. "I shall have even greater respect for your mama, knowing this."

My face fell and I pushed my bonnet forward a little to shade my eyes. "It did not end as one might have wished. The watch was called and all of them were dragged before a magistrate. The men insisted that the women had led them on, and my mother was forced to tell the whole story. It was a great scandal and was even written about in all the papers."

"I see."

I could tell that he did. "Of course Mama was in complete disgrace, even though sensible people knew her actions were perfectly innocent. But there are always people who will make more of a scandal than there really is. What made matters worse was that the Earl of Stonebridge wrote one of his infamous letters to the newspapers about the incident. He suspected that my father intended to marry my mother in spite of the hoopla, and he tried to shame Papa out of it. Nothing of the sort! My father was not so fainthearted, you may be sure. He offered for her the very next day. And not out of pity! He had already determined upon it, and this only further convinced him to act."

"Your father must have been a brave man to take on such an unconventional miss."

The hedges alongside the road swayed in the summer breeze, and a whitethroat fluttered in and out, singing its gushing, jerky little song. "He loved her dearly, but I think it was not so easy for him to live with her wild starts. My recollections, even as a child, are of him gently but firmly insisting that Mama behave with more discretion. Sometimes I think they might both have been a little less proscribed in their behavior if they had not had their family so soon. Mama has often remarked on how very responsible Papa became when Robert was born. Before that . . . Well, Mama says that there was just the tiniest bit of wildness to him, in those early days. Papa's lessons in decorum worked with Amanda, but with me they didn't take so well. I fear I've inherited a bit of my mother's nature.''

I shrugged and gave him a rueful little grin. "I don't think Mama minds so much that I haven't Amanda's uprightness. And I know Papa loved me, even when he didn't approve of things I did. So it's worked out all right, except during my Season. Everyone was waiting for me to do something outrageous. Actually, I behaved quite within reason—as even my father would have told you. It was just that the earl wrote another of his letters to the newspaper . . .''

Sir John's brow furrowed with annoyance. "Surely not. What could he possibly have had to say?"

"Poor Robert. The burden fell on him. Though the earl hinted that my father had no control over me, the letter was more of a tirade about my brother lacking the proper background to ascend to such distinction as he would one day. Stonebridge always believed that he would outlive my father, but he knew that chances of his providing his own heir were nil by then. So he attacked Robert's character and diligence.''

Sir John snorted. "There's no question which of them is the truer gentleman. But Robert does seem to have allowed himself to be in the old fellow's pocket since then. I've noticed that myself.''

"Each time he's come down to visit us, there has been a letter to the newspaper. The earl's last one was about our missing horse. It's a threat Stonebridge holds over my brother, that he will make him and our family even greater objects of ridicule if Robert doesn't toe the line. I've tried to assure him that it doesn't matter so much, but he's convinced that Amanda and I will never find suitable husbands if our name is continually dragged through the parlors of London as a source of amusement and scandal. If the earl continues his mean-spirited attacks on us, I'm convinced Robert won't ever come down to visit at all. As the earl gets older, he becomes more and more unbalanced. I hate to think that his threat will hang over Robert's head until the old geezer sticks his spoon in the wall.''

For a long moment Sir John said nothing. Perhaps he was remembering the *ton*'s delight with the last published letter. Robert had been chagrined almost beyond words. Mocking his management of his horses was a most vulnerable spot with him. I was sure Sir John knew that. His expression was thoughtful. ''I'm glad you told me,'' he said finally. ''He's never commented on it, though I've wondered why . . . But I may be able to find a way to ease his situation.''

''I do hope so.''

Suddenly I noticed that we were almost to the turn off the Newmarket Road. Unfortunately there was a long procession of cows blocking our path. Sir John drew his horses to a complete halt, and though they fidgeted with nervous energy, he paid little attention to them. His attention was entirely on me. Those insistent eyes studied my face, taking in every detail. I could feel the tension grow between us, as it had that day beside the pond. Good-humored, and even wry, he had been, but he had stubbornly refused to go away.

His eyes now seemed to glow with the warmth he had shown them, and I felt myself catching it, a little. My cheeks grew hot as he continued to gaze into my eyes, and my breathing started to catch slightly. He lifted a gauntleted finger to brush back the hair that had slipped out from under my bonnet. ''You're a lovely woman,'' he said. ''And quite remarkable. That sharp tongue and that soft heart are a potent combination. No wonder you found none of the London blades up to your weight.''

The warmth had spread from my cheeks down to my chest. I was so very close to him that I could almost feel his skin next to mine. His continued gaze unsettled me. Why was he doing this? There was no laughter in him now. Yet his concentration on me was total.

The cows had long since disappeared in the direction of Cambridge. I cleared my throat and reminded him. He set his pair moving again, without a word. I gave directions when necessary. Otherwise, we said nothing. There were things that we might have said, that our bodies seemed to be saying to each other, that were not possible to speak aloud. Alarmed, I tried not to listen, but my body was as attuned to him as an ear to music.

·7·

Mr. Hinchly was his inhospitable self. I'd often wondered whether he had become that way from living in the most inhospitable farmhouse I had ever seen, or whether he had chosen the building because it suited his temperament. Like the farm buildings in the west, his had originally been a longhouse where farmer shared space with animal. Though the building had long since been converted to solely human use, it still looked cramped and unwelcoming, with its tiny windows and blackened bricks. Mr. Hinchly could have afforded to build himself a fine manor house, but apparently had never had the least desire to do so.

I had sent a note informing him of our proposed visit and had received no word in reply. "He sort of grunted," Jed informed me. His welcome consisted of an offhand remark about Sir John's horses—"Got 'em from a good man, I see."—before he stumped off toward the stables, apparently expecting us to follow. Sir John handed me down from the curricle.

"Friendly sort of fellow, isn't he?" he whispered under cover of our horses being led away.

"I warned you. For him, this is positively affable. Sometimes when Robert and I used to come, he only met us at the stables after we'd investigated each of the horses."

"But you assured me that you could handle him."

86

"And so I can. For one thing, you have to understand that he won't deal at all with strangers." I was walking rapidly to keep up with him. "Unless he has an introduction to a buyer, he won't let one of his horses go off."

"Very odd in him." Sir John regarded the retreating form with interest. "Doesn't that hamper him a bit in making a profit from his breeding?"

"Not at all. In this neighborhood he's extremely well known and can't produce enough horses to satisfy the demand. So don't expect to get away easily with one of his finer pairs. He'll charge you dearly for anything you show a real interest in."

"I'll remember."

And he did. At most stables it's difficult to find all the really necessary qualities in a pair. One will be truly noble, with strong loins and a perfect disposition, while the other is a most inferior animal. But Sir John was particularly interested in spirit and metal, so color, shape, and height were secondary considerations. A pair will look more beautifully matched if their paces suit well and they have an equal strength than if their markings are identical.

Because of my special sensibility with regard to Sir John, I could tell when an animal interested him, though there was no overt sign Mr. Hinchly would necessarily have noticed. As we watched the animals put through their paces, I saw that Sir John was excited about the bays, and what magnificent animals they were! Strong firm necks, full broad breasts, short-jointed, strong-backed. They would have been my choice over the creams or the blacks.

Sir John looked at a dozen pairs, questioning Hinchly on their breeding and their price. Only once did he refer to the bays, by saying, "I suppose my mother could use them for her phaeton."

Mr. Hinchly may not have been taken in by this

ploy, but he couldn't be sure of Sir John's interest, either. Less showy than the baronet's chestnuts, or even a dappled pair that he could have had at Overview, the bays were superb in their movement and speed. Sir John seemed especially interested in their speed.

"It may be that I could use the bays," he said, "but I'm not certain. Perhaps I'll take a few days to think it over."

Mr. Hinchly merely grunted at him. "Don't make no matter to me. Might miss them, though. Another fellow were lookin' at them yesterday. Darndest thing how no one can make up his mind these days. What do you say, Miss Ryder?"

"Oh, I'd take them. A fine pair. But I think you're asking a little more than they deserve for their ages, Mr. Hinchly. It could be that they won't live up to their early promise."

Sir John blinked at me, but Mr. Hinchly looked chagrined. There had been word that one of his horses had shown to less advantage a year after he'd been purchased. Not Hinchly's fault, of course, but something to use as a bargaining point, if you knew about it.

"Now that weren't none of my doing, miss," he grumbled. "Probably that Connerly fellow didn't take the care that he should have. That horse had as much promise as any I've bred in the last ten years."

"I realize that. Which is why I would introduce a note of caution to my friend Sir John. Not that he wouldn't take the best possible care of your horses. But they're young, and it's a bit of a gamble when one is counting on them living up to especially high expectations."

Hinchly considered this for a moment while Sir John made noises about wanting to get me alone to discuss the matter. I agreed to walk off with him to stand under the sycamore trees along the carriage path. "Are you saying they'll not do?" he demanded.

"Not at all. They're spectacular. I just think you might bargain a little with him if you knew about this recent episode."

"Would you buy them?"

"In a minute—if I had the need and means. Which I'm sure you do." I smiled kindly on him; he was, in fact, asking my advice, wasn't he?

"These are for me, not for your brother. I haven't decided what to do about his request yet."

"Offer Hinchly twenty guineas less than he's asking and settle for fifteen less. That shouldn't be a problem."

"But they're worth what he's asking."

"In town, perhaps, but not in the country. You'd pay less where you usually buy, wouldn't you?"

"Yes." He ran long fingers through his thick brown hair and shook his head. "I don't want to put his back up, Miss Ryder."

"Trust me."

Though he looked dubious, he followed my advice when we returned to an impatient Hinchly. The old man would have had less respect for him if he hadn't tried to bargain, but it was hard to tell that by his gruff, obstinate appearance. There's nothing Hinchly likes more than dickering over the price of a horse, and he'll continue the argument for weeks if one isn't too impatient to be off. That's how I got Mama's Antelope, though no one seems to understand how delicate a negotiation it was, because Hinchly really wanted to keep the horse for his wife's use. I bribed his wife with some of Mrs. Cooper's raspberry tarts. Mrs. Hinchly is not overfond of riding, much like my sister.

Sir John and I left the farm in good spirits. He felt that he'd done a good bargaining job, and he was more than pleased with the pair of gleaming bays, which would be sent over to Hastings the next day. I decided to take advantage of his exuberance.

"Why don't you let me drive the curricle to our picnic spot?" I asked when we were out of sight of Hinchly Farms. I knew he wouldn't wish old Hinchly to see me driving the carriage, though Hinchly would have thought nothing of it, if truth were told. I'd driven there before.

My companion regarded me with astonishment. "You don't understand what I've told you. The curricle is finely balanced, and my horses are testy with another hand on their reins. We would only come to grief, my dear Miss Ryder."

"Oh, I doubt anything so awful would happen. You would be sitting right here, able to take the reins from me in a moment. The road is perfectly straight until we reach the turnoff. Do let me have a chance."

"Your brother told me you would pester me, and he assured me that you were able to handle most anything, but he could not possibly have been thinking of my chestnuts." Sir John regarded me with a creased forehead. "Why would you want to drive them?"

"The challenge," I admitted. "They're strong and the carriage is, as you say, precariously balanced. It would be the greatest challenge I've had in driving so far."

He snorted. "And you think I should be the one to indulge your further education, do you? Not a bit of it, my girl. I haven't the slightest desire to find myself in a ditch—or worse."

I pouted. Yes, I know it is unbecoming of one with my spirit, but I did it anyway.

He hesitated and cast a strange glance at me, almost as though he had no power to refuse my request, though many men have done so. After a moment he shrugged his broad shoulders and nodded. "Very well. See that you don't overturn us."

To be honest, I was more than a little frightened. Oh, I wanted to drive the carriage, but it would be difficult. I pulled off my gloves and pulled on the gauntlets he indicated that were stuffed in a side pocket of the vehicle. They were miles too big for my hands, but that wasn't what bothered me about them. Stuffing my hand into them was like losing my hands in his, which made me feel flushed. When I made no move to take the reins, he laughed and asked, "Lost your nerve, have you?"

"Certainly not!" I shifted slightly closer to him as he slowed the beasts and made ready to transfer the leather thongs. I could feel my heart in my throat, pounding frantically. But once I had my hands on the reins, I felt not a second's hesitation. There is something truly thrilling about driving a fine pair; it is like nothing else in the world. I could feel their restlessness under my lighter touch but they immediately picked up speed again. Sir John kept a close eye on all of this.

His thighs were now hard against mine and I could feel the tension in him, ready to move in for the slightest cause. On the way over we had passed several dogs who barked wildly and chased after us. Though his horses showed disdain, they also acted slightly skittish. Sir John had hardly seemed to notice. But he did now.

A spotted brown-and-white mongrel charged up a path and appeared ready to lunge himself at the nearest horse. Growling fiercely, he ran back and forth in front of the hedgerow as we rapidly approached. I could tell he was a fearless thing and too stupid to know better than to get under the horses' hooves. My mind was set on protecting the horses, devil take the dog.

"You'd best give me the reins," Sir John snapped.

"It will be all right," I said, just as one of the horses tossed its head and broke stride. "Here, just put your hands over mine. They'll settle from your touch."

And indeed they did. For myself, the reaction was just the opposite. His firm grip on my hands made my heart start to hammer. The pup was soon left behind, but Sir John continued to hold my hands. His arms pressed against mine and I felt as though I was practically in his lap. Just the way Papa had taught us each to drive when we were very small, sitting in his lap with our hands on the reins and his over them. But this was different: being so close to Sir John was disturbing.

"We're coming to the turnoff for our picnic spot," I advised him, gently withdrawing myself from his pseudo-embrace, leaving him in possession of his horses. "On the left there, by the clump of oaks, the road turns toward a lovely stream."

For once, driving a fine pair of horses was not uppermost in my mind. My breathing was coming quickly, almost as if I'd been running, and I couldn't understand what was happening. That spot of trouble had made me tense, but it was long past. Neither the baronet nor I said a word as he drove down the tree-shaded lane. When I motioned toward a sun-dappled spot along the bank of a cheerfully babbling brook, he mused, "It reminds me of your hidden pond."

If he hadn't said it, I don't think I would have become so self-conscious. But feeling as I did at the moment and having him remind me of my naked swim and his delighted spying up on me . . . Well, I began to feel goosebumps all over me. He climbed down from the carriage and offered me his hands.

I had already disposed of his gauntlets, reluctantly, and now offered my hand to him. His grip was firm and no more insinuating than it should have been. Still, when I stood on the grassy ground, my knees did not believe they were well-supported. A flutter in my breast so distracted me that I could barely look at him. I moistened my lips and said, "If you'll hand down the picnic basket, I'll set things out."

Mrs. Cooper had packed a wonderful assortment. Sir John murmured his appreciation as I unearthed the wine and settled it in the stream. While I spread the other items out on a cloth, I caught his eye on me more than once, a puzzled, almost alarmed look in the blue depths. Nervous, I kept up a running commentary.

"These tarts are not as good as the raspberry, but I think you will like them. And the chicken is so tender it will melt in your mouth. Mrs. Cooper has the idea that a meal should be either hot or cold, and not tepid as ours will be, but she makes allowances for al fresco dining. See all the cheeses? Just the sort of thing she would think most appropriate. I suppose you noticed that Amanda doesn't care much for cheeses. I think it is because she was made to help with them when she was young and she took a great dislike to the dairy." And so forth. Not an intelligent word in the bunch, but I couldn't seem to help myself.

His presence unnerved and captivated me. I began to notice the very intense blue of his eyes, and the rough texture of the skin on his forearms, where he had pushed up his sleeves. His lips seemed unbearably close to my face, somehow, though they were no closer than was proper. They looked so terribly tempting. Now, I had kissed a few young men. It was not that a kiss was a totally unknown thing to me. And yet, I felt breathless with the desire to kiss him, to lock my lips against his.

"Do have some of the pigeon pie," I offered. "It's one of Mrs. Cooper's specialties."

He made no move to take anything from me, or to do anything else, for that matter. His eyes were so

entrancing that I found myself sitting there stunned. I
think I shivered with the force of my desire to press
myself against his chest, to kiss him, to touch his skin.
I don't know how long we sat that way, staring at each
other. And yet he said nothing.

Finally, he took a piece of chicken. Took it and
brought it to his lips, tasting the smallest bit, before
offering it to me, right at my lips. It was as intimate
as a kiss, and yet not satisfying. My hands fluttered
uneasily in my lap.

When he spoke, I barely recognized his voice. Ordinarily he had a rather sophisticated drawl. Now his
voice was rough with intensity. "I had never seen a
woman swimming naked before. You were a vision of
graceful innocence. But I'm far from innocent and you
have no idea of the fleshly desires such a sight can
inspire."

"Don't I?" I said it softly, but I wanted him to hear.
When he made no further move toward me, I added,
"I'm not totally innocent, you know. I've kissed sev-
eral gentlemen in my life."

An amused skepticism appeared on his charming
countenance. "There's kissing and there's kissing,"
he said. "I doubt if you've really been kissed."

"Well, of course I have!"

He moved closer to me. "Then perhaps I should
show you the potential dangers. There are dangers,
dear Catherine. Kissing can lead to the most astonishing feelings."

Suddenly his lips were on mine and I discovered
immediately that he was right. I was feeling something
quite different than I had experienced before. For one
thing, those other men hadn't the slightest knowledge
of how to kiss properly. Well, actually, they weren't
men at all, but neighborhood boys I'd known my whole
life.

Sir John knew how to kiss. He didn't kiss you like

your mother did before you went to bed at night, as some of the boys had. And he didn't try to crush his mouth against mine in an urgency only likely to bruise my lips. His lips were so astonishingly delicious that I could barely believe anything could taste so good. They were soft and firm, warm and startlingly icy. He played along my lips with a motion that rubbed and teased, tasting me and tempting me. Within moments my breathlessness increased, to say nothing of the turbulence that rose in me and threatened to overtake me entirely. My body went through wild fluctuations of heat and cold. After a moment I was forced to pull back.

"You see?" His eyes held mine with glowing intensity. "There is a great deal of danger in kissing, Catherine. Do you feel the temptation?"

My name on his lips gave me gooseflesh. There was a roughness to the way he said it that roused an excitement in me with which I was totally unfamiliar. It made me feel almost cross with him. "I'm not in danger of giving in to temptation," I informed him crisply. "You don't need to think you can toy with me just to teach me a lesson. I'm sure I'm no different than any other young woman of my upbringing."

"Now there I think you are quite wrong. Most young ladies have the temptation bred out of them."

"You needn't make sport with me, Sir John. I may not be as meek as a country schoolgirl or as sophisticated as a London mistress, but I am the happier for it. Not for me whiling away every day going to parties and wearing fine dresses."

His hands moved to my sides, almost as if he were attempting to measure me. I felt I could while away a few hours just with them there. "How do you spend your time? Other than swimming, that is?"

I colored. "I ride and drive, and I walk and read, and I help Mama and Amanda run the household, as well as doing my share of the parish chores and the visiting of the estate sick or injured. It's the country life, and I am more than content with it. What use is there in flirting with a group of silly men and gossiping with insipid misses?''

''I certainly can't think of any.'' His hands moved ever so slightly upward and I could feel my breathing increase. My heart pounded harder, too, and I was sure he must feel it, if not hear it. ''How did you learn to swim?'' he asked.

''Oh, Papa taught Robert, and Robert taught me.'' At his startled look, I added, ''We were very young then. You needn't act the prude for my benefit.''

''You're quite right. But I could help you improve your swimming style.'' His hands smoothed the fabric over my back, gliding up to my shoulders. ''You need to lift your arms completely over your head, to get the most powerful stroke. You were just paddling along, which will keep you afloat, but won't take you any distance. Like this.''

Instead of showing me by lifting his own arm over his head, he took hold of mine, both of them, and lifted them one at a time over my head. It was a strange sensation. With my arms that high over my head, the gown stretched tight across my bust. He brought the arms up again in a rhythm that made my heart pound hard.

''And you turn your head, like this, to breathe,'' he explained. This time he moved his own head, inhaling to the side and blowing out when he put his head down. My eyes were locked on his mouth, pursed and ready for air—or for a kiss. ''Try it,'' he said.

I felt like a fool, with him watching me that way. He urged me to use my arms and try the breathing at the same time. ''Good, good,'' he encouraged me as I followed his example. Suddenly his lips were there at my breathing-out place and he brushed mine lightly, not quite a kiss. I was so shaken that I paused; he insisted that I must keep up the rhythm or lose my chance to learn how to do it properly.

Nonsense, of course, but I did as he said. Each time my mouth reached its apex, his lips were there, gently urging me on. His hands were high on my sides, in an effort to keep me in a more-or-less horizontal position, I suppose. All I could think of was that they were so close to my breasts, and for some reason I had an overwhelming need for him to touch me there. He didn't. And my body ached for something more, something to relieve the inner tension that was building inside me.

"You've got it," he said in that soft, rough voice of his. "You're a quick learner, but it's different out of water. Tomorrow we could go to the pond . . ."

"Don't be ridiculous!" Though I meant it to sound determined, my words came out totally lacking in conviction. I could indeed picture myself in the pond, practicing my swimming, with his hands on my naked body, supporting me, his lips rewarding my efforts. In fact, I felt naked just sitting there beside him. My shallow breathing increased once again when he drew me to him and held me in a tight embrace, his lips firm on mine, his own heart hammering against my breast.

"What would be the harm in it?" he whispered. "It's not as though I hadn't already seen you . . . in that condition. I promise you I would not behave in any way that you disliked."

I moistened my lips and drew back from him. "It's out of the question. You would have to swim without your clothes, and I don't think I should see you without your clothes, any more than you should see me. You shouldn't have seen me the other day."

"But I did." I felt his hands run down my back, farther than I should have liked, except that I did.

''Your skin glowed like alabaster in the water. I could see every womanly curve of you. And your face. I don't think I shall ever forget the look on your face when you became aware of me.''

He laughed with a charming ruefulness. ''I didn't wish to alarm you, but it was beyond my powers of abstinence to leave before I had to. I should have known then who you were. Your swimming fit quite well with what I'd heard of you in London. A truly spirited young woman. I think that was half the reason I agreed to come here.''

''What was the other half?''

He frowned and shook his head, as though to free it from some distraction. ''Why, to buy the horses, of course. Why else would I have come?''

I had broken the spell that surrounded us. He drew back from me, his hands leaving my body slowly, but completely. He picked up a chunk of bread and spread it with the golden butter Mrs. Cooper had sent in a crock. ''I'm starved,'' he admitted. ''We should get on with our meal, don't you think?''

I didn't agree one bit, but I pretended that I did. With fingers that still shook slightly, I chose an orange and began to peel it. Sir John wasn't looking at me then. He retrieved the wine from its cooling place and expertly wielded the corkscrew. I could picture him doing this dozens of times, on dozens of picnics, with dozens of voluptuous women. Not all at the same time, of course. When he spoke, it took me a moment to bring my wandering attention back to where we were.

''Have you heard about the highwayman who's been working the Newmarket Road?''

Several people had been held up at pistol-point by a highwayman over the last few weeks, but there was surprisingly little talk of the matter. Not that it was a common occurrence in our neighborhood. There hadn't been so much as a robbery on the high road for a good ten years before this.

"There have been murmurings," I admitted. "I daresay our constable will manage to catch the fellow one of these days, as he doesn't seem to have much sense about who he waylays. Lord Ekton was robbed last week, and though he's a wretched human being, he's rich as may be, and usually has several outriders with him. Lucky for the highwayman that his lordship happened to be riding alone instead of in his carriage."

"Lord Ekton is only one of several people who have come under attack from the fellow. I myself was robbed a fortnight ago."

"A fortnight ago?" I was astonished. "I had no idea you were in this area a fortnight ago."

"I was coming from the Newmarket races and I have to admit it sounded the most colossal nonsense when someone yelled, 'Stand and deliver!' At first I couldn't even see the fellow. He was hidden behind some rocks to the side of the road. But he meant business and insisted on my purse."

He was pouring wine into my glass, but his eyes were on me. "And you gave it over?" I asked.

"Of course. I would far rather lose a few pounds than have a bullet through my skull, Miss Ryder. Perhaps you would have preferred the latter fate for me."

"Not at all." Though I have to admit it seemed rather tame of him to hand over his purse without a struggle. I said as much.

"Well," he said, his eyes full of mischief, "perhaps I would have put up more resistance if I'd been alone. But the highwayman was waving his pistol most menacingly at my charming companion."

I might have known: he had been with his mistress. Suddenly I felt so dispirited that I took an enormous gulp of the wine, forgetting everything that Mrs. Cooper had told me.

Sir John shook his head in a disparaging sort of way. "You really shouldn't swill it down that way, my dear. It's quite a decent wine."

I was torn between wishing to toss the rest of it in his face and "swilling" it down my own throat. In the end I managed to knock it over, so I ignored him and helped myself to more food as consolation.

·8·

Amanda awaited our return in the side garden. Sir John made for her like a bee to a
flower. He didn't have to desert me so rapidly after he
handed me down from the curricle. Obviously he was
a very fickle fellow. I hurried into the house to have a
word with Mama.

She was in the summer parlor gazing absently at the
open door. I could tell she wasn't in one of her
"states," though, because she looked up when I entered, and smiled. "Did you have a nice day, my
sweet?" she asked.

"Nothing out of the ordinary," I declared. What a
liar I could be. "Sir John bought a handsome pair of
bays. He's with Amanda in the arbor now, you will be
pleased to know."

Her brow puckered. "Why should I be pleased about
that?"

"I can see that you are determined to marry them
off. And the more time he spends with her, the more
likely that eventuality will become."

Mama gave a charming laugh. "It seems to me he's
spending just as much time with you as he is with
Amanda. I've known men to do that before. Unable to
make up their minds between two delightful sisters."

"Oh, I doubt if that is Sir John's problem," I said.
"Besides, he spends very little time with me."

"That's not how Amanda sees it. She said that he

101

often goes off to consult with you, or walk with you, or sit in the arbor. And then there was your drive to-day, with a picnic. Oh, yes, I think we shall have to consider him smitten with the both of you.'' She brushed her hands briskly down her skirts. ''Which is probably no real help, so far as finding each of you a husband is concerned. He will doubtless take off for London after a while, simply to escape his confusion.''

I could easily believe he would leave. If Mama couldn't see how much he was making up to Amanda, then Sir John was keeping it from her. The sly devil. And he convinced Amanda that he was, to some extent, making up to me. Decidedly there was something suspicious going on and I had a burning desire to discover what it was. Tonight I would wait, not in the hall, but in the downstairs passage that he would have to traverse to leave the house.

I made sure that there was a candle burning in the passage so that I would be able to see any trespasser clearly. As one came down the back stairs, there was a tread that creaked so loudly it would give me a chance to move farther under the table where I had placed my blankets. This time no one was going to leave without my seeing who it was.

It was a wretchedly uncomfortable bed I made my-self, but I did manage to doze off once or twice. Then, at a little after midnight I heard the sharp crack of the noisy tread. I drew back so that only my head re-mained visible. Anyone leaving the house would have to swing almost full around to see me. The step on the stairs was light and sure, as if this person had trod them many times before. The door at the foot of the stairs swung open as though there were not the least need for caution.

But the person who emerged was cloaked from head

to toe in an enormous black cape and wore riding boots. For a fraction of a second the face seemed to turn slightly, and to my astonishment I saw that this nighttime adventurer was wearing a black mask. A mask, for heaven's sake! I meant to cry out, but something prevented me and the fellow was gone, the door closing sharply after.

The only thing I could be sure of was that it hadn't been Sir John. The masked person was not nearly tall enough. And yet, who else could it be? The only other people staying in the house were Cousin Bret, Mama, and Amanda. That it could conceivably be one of the servants hardly occurred to me. Our servants would not so much as borrow a horse from the stables without permission, and this masked adventurer was obviously intent on riding out.

I was struggling with this dilemma when a second noise came from the stairs. Not that the stair creaked. Apparently this person knew how to avoid the noisy tread and was already pushing open the door slowly and soundlessly. I drew back under the rim of the table again and strained to see who had appeared.

There was no mistaking the size and solidity of him. And I saw his face as he turned to close the door silently before his long strides carried him swiftly through the passage. He had disappeared in a matter of seconds, though he hardly seemed to hasten. In the candlelight his face had looked extraordinarily determined and intelligent, lacking the lighthearted frivolity with which he was wont to regard Amanda and me during the days.

It was only then that I realized my mistake. The most logical place for me to have positioned myself would have been in the tack room of the stables. One or both of these people intended to ride out, and I was way behind them now, trying to pull on my boots and fetch up my riding jacket over my nightclothes. I was determined to follow them even though I had lost a lot of time.

With a sort of desperation, I slipped out the back door, running down the path toward the stables. I could see and hear nothing in the black stillness of the night. If there were hoofbeats, I didn't hear them. I could only hear the pounding of my heart and the scuffle of my boots on the gravel path.

There was no light on in the stables. The door, I could see even from a distance, was closed. But I had no difficulty in opening it. Our coachman didn't believe in barring the door, in case of fire. He was insistent that no one would dare come in to steal a horse with himself and his staff so close by. I let myself in and waited a moment for my eyes to adjust further to the dark.

Nothing broke the silence except the shifting of an animal in its stall somewhere down the line. And yet I wondered if there wasn't someone else in the dark with me there. I could almost feel a presence, lurking in one of the stalls, or a loose box, or even in the tack room. It was not that I felt frightened, merely that I was aware of a prickling on my neck that was like hackles rising. I had every right to be there; whether my invisible companion did or not remained to be seen.

As I walked down the length of stalls, I checked to see which horses were missing. The first horse not in its stall was Mama's Antelope. My own Lofty seemed to sense my presence, for she lifted her head and whinnied softly, moving to thrust her head over the wooden gate for my attention. Without thinking, I reached up to rub her forehead, right on the spot she most approves of.

Sir John's Apollo was missing, which didn't surprise me, of course. And Robert's Thunder. No other horses were gone. Not that three wasn't quite enough! I hurried to the back entrance and opened the door a few inches, but there was nothing to be seen. Sir John and the Masked Rider were long gone.

I stood there pondering what I should do. My chances of encountering someone if I waited in the stables were reasonably good, but it might be hours and I was already shivering in my nightclothes, despite the riding coat. So I decided to return to the house to contemplate my next move.

Disgruntled, I made my way back to the house and started to gather up my blankets from under the table. I was so jumpy by this time that I was starting to hear all sorts of creaks and groans in the old house. Once I thought I heard the stair creak again, and I slid under the table so fast I grazed my head on one of the leg corners. This caused a great deal of pain and, as I soon discovered, had drawn blood as well. It didn't help that the noise turned out to be a false alarm.

By the time I had trudged up the stairs my head was pounding abominably. I couldn't bear to think about who the Masked Rider might be, since no matter who he was, it was going to mean trouble for us. I kept trying to remember if Cousin Bret had been here long enough to be the guilty party, but my aching head wouldn't obey me. The only hope, it seemed to me, was that the villain was a friend of one of our servants, hiding out in our house, but somehow that seemed terribly unlikely.

A drop of blood splashed onto my hand as I reached the upper landing. I've always been a bit squeamish about the sight of blood and this blob made me feel slightly faint. In the hall closet I found a plaster for my head, and in my room I rinsed the cut with water from my ewer. The cut smarted like anything, and it bled profusely for some time. That's what scalp wounds will do, and I felt rather ill by the time the flow had been stanched. The cut was back of my hairline and with luck no one would notice it in the morning.

Exhausted and depressed, I climbed into my bed, drew the covers up to my chin, and tried to forget that my aching crown was only one of the headaches that faced me. Mercifully, I quickly lost consciousness.

In the morning it took me a matter of moments to wrap myself in a robe and slide my feet into slippers. My knock on Mama's door was soft to the point of being hardly a sound at all, but she called out in a firm cheerful voice, "Come in!"

She probably thought I was her maid bringing chocolate, but she didn't by the flicker of an eyelash show that she was surprised by my arrival. Nothing seemed the least suspicious or out of place in her room. I don't know if I expected to find a black cape tossed over a chair or a mask on the dressing table. "Why, Catherine, dear, what a surprise to see you at this hour. Is something the matter?"

Closing the door carefully behind me, since I had no way of knowing if any of the others were abroad, I nodded and took up a position at the end of her dressing table, where she was seated. "Mama," I began, wondering how someone had this sort of conversation with her mother, "I was in the back hallway last night."

"Were you, dear?" she asked absently as she tucked a wisp of graying hair behind her ear. "Whatever were you doing there?"

"Well, I was intent on finding out what Sir John is really up to, but that doesn't seem to be as important now as what else is going on."

She turned her head so that her eyes met mine directly, rather than in the mirror. "What *is* going on, dear?"

"Someone in this household is a highwayman," I

announced with my natural flare for drama. "I saw it with my own eyes, a figure come down the back stairs dressed in a black cape, with a mask. And then there was Sir John, who followed that person out of the house."

"Did he?" I could tell she was startled. Then a small frown drew together the brown brows that usually made perfect crescents over her eyes. "Why would he do such a thing?"

"Well, because he wishes to find out who is going out to rob innocent people on the high road," I said. "And, Mama, there is no ignoring the fact that it must be one of three people: Amanda, Cousin Bret, or . . . you."

She gave a cheerful laugh. "Now, now, dear. You are exaggerating. Or perhaps you are suffering from a nightmare that seemed extremely real to you. I'm not surprised that you dream of Sir John. No doubt he's very much on your mind."

"This was no dream," I insisted. "And it's a very serious matter, Mama."

"Well, I don't see how you can expect me to take seriously the idea that your sister is a highwayman. I've never heard anything so ludicrous."

"Not Amanda specifically. Though it could have been her, I agree that it is highly unlikely. Which leaves only Cousin Bret . . . and you." It was hard for me to press her this way, but it had to be done.

Mama cocked her head to one side, as though considering the matter. "I don't believe your Cousin Bret is quite brave enough to be a highwayman. If you see what I mean. After all, someone might actually point a pistol at him or laugh in his face. No, I shouldn't think it would be your cousin, either."

What was she saying? I could feel a shiver race down my spine. With the utmost fortitude I drew a deep breath and asked, "And was it you, Mama?"

A tinkling laugh escaped her. I hadn't heard that

happy sound since before my father died. "Really, Catherine, is it likely that your poor, aged mother would do such a wild, unprincipled thing? You are grasping at straws, my dear. One of the servants may be up to some mischief, but I doubt very much that he would be a highwayman. That doesn't sound at all like any of our dear helpers, does it? It was probably some costume meant to impress one of the maids."

Not a likely scenario, by my lights. I would have pressed her on the point, except that she had turned to stare at herself in the mirror, caught up in the perusal of the crinkles at the edges of her eyes.

"Am I such an old-looking woman?" she asked. "Your father always made me feel so young that I never thought much about aging. And yet here I am, with these cracks in my face, and my sagging neck, and my graying hair. Do you suppose I will die soon?"

Astonished, I gave her a startled shake. "Don't talk that way! Whyever would you die? You're healthy and not the least bit old, for heaven's sake."

"Harold died. He wasn't old either."

"But his heart was bad. You know the doctor said his heart was bad."

"Perhaps my heart is bad," she suggested, almost hopefully. "Perhaps there is some disease even now eating away at me. That's possible, you know. Mrs. Standon was eaten up inside that way. She just shriveled up and died. It only took three months." She gazed off into the distance. "I could be gone in three months."

"You're not going to die!"

"Well, of course I'm going to die. Everyone dies. Don't be such a ninny."

"You're not going to die *soon*," I shouted. When Mother was in one of these moods, it was hard to get things through to her, and one was always tempted to shout. It did no good, of course, but I seemed always to manage to do it anyhow.

"Hush! You'll disturb the whole household. And frighten your sister. Amanda doesn't know I'm going to die."

"You are *not* going to die!" I whispered this time, but fiercely. "You're perfectly healthy, and you're just trying to avoid answering my questions. This is very important."

"Is it?" She still sounded vague. "I shouldn't think anything would make much difference, since I will no doubt be dead soon. But I shall come and talk to you, my dear, when you need comforting. As my friends do, and your father. So many people are afraid of ghosts. You needn't be, you know. They only come to keep you company, to give you advice, sometimes. If you think I would be of no use to you, of course, you must simply tell me." She brought her head up sharply, eyeing me as if I'd given her offense. "I don't wish to be where I'm not wanted."

"Mama, you must stop this playacting. There's something very much amiss here and I must get to the bottom of it. Do you know what you did last night?"

She blinked at me as though I had lost my mind. "Well, of course I know what I did last night. Do you think I've lost my mind?"

Just then we were interrupted by Amanda, who wandered in, clutching her head. "Oh, Mama," she said in the most pitiful voice. "I have the most abominable headache. Could you give me one of your powders for it?"

Mama began to fuss around her, completely ignoring me, except to say, "Why don't you run along now, Catherine? I'll be with your sister for a while."

With a despairing shake of my head, I left.

At least Amanda was out of the way for a while. Not that I didn't feel sorry for her when she had the headache, but she seemed to milk it for all it was worth. Besides, she was much more interested in my mother's sympathy than in mine. Anyhow, I got dressed and went down to the breakfast room, where I found Sir John seated in lonely splendor, as it were.

He rose when I entered and held a chair for me, with just the tiniest trace of a smile on his lips. "How pleasant to have you join me," he remarked as he resumed his seat. "Usually your mother and sister are here before you."

"They won't be down this morning; Amanda isn't feeling well and Mama is taking care of her."

"I'm sorry to hear of her illness. I hope it isn't something serious."

"Merely the headache. Apparently it is very painful for a few hours and then gradually disappears. Nothing she can't handle," I added callously, not wanting him to think Amanda was some sort of weakling. "Robert used to have it occasionally, I recall, but I don't seem prone to it myself."

"Nor I. We must be the lucky ones." This time he most decidedly smiled at me in that intimate way he had. "Perhaps you'll ride out with me this morning."

"I should have thought your horse had had enough exercise already."

"I beg your pardon?"

"Well, it's not for me to tell you that it's dangerous to be dashing about unfamiliar countryside in the dead of night, but if you have a thought to your horse, you wouldn't do it."

His brows were lowered rather grimly over hooded eyes. "I'm afraid I don't understand you, Miss Ryder."

"I saw you leave the house last night and discovered that your horse was gone from the stable. Why did you go out?"

"If you followed me," he said, sounding highly dubious, "You must know very well why I went out."

So that was how he was going to play the game. Well, I knew some evasions of my own and could use them when the circumstances dictated it. "You mean because of the Masked Rider? You mustn't let that sort of prank mislead you. Once a year the servants get up to this trick and no matter how we try to discourage them, they will have their fun."

"How very imaginative of you! Did that just come to your mind, or is it something you worked on all night?"

The hateful fellow! He had the most annoying grin on his lips. I wished to wipe it off instantly, so I said, "I suppose it might have been your own servant, of course. He seems a rather suspicious fellow."

"You're not going to cozzen me with these farradiddles. Don't forget, Miss Ryder, that I was robbed by this Masked Rider of yours, and I can tell you that there was nothing about the person I saw last night that differed from my impression of the person who robbed me."

"Oh, how could you tell?" I scoffed. "It was probably dark when you were made to stand and deliver, and I daresay you were more than a little distracted by your friend. Your impression of the highwayman was doubtless very meager."

Sir John pushed his chair back slightly from the table and replaced his napkin by his knife. "Tell me something. Why are you so determined to make me believe that no one in this household has anything to do with the highwayman? Do you suspect that there actually is some connection?"

"Devil a bit," I muttered. "What I suspect is that you came here for some other reason than to buy a pair for your carriage. Why don't you tell me what that reason was? Perhaps then we'd be able to deal better together."

He sat for some time with a worried expression on

his face, a bit of his lip caught between his teeth. It was a habit I'd noticed once before and found rather endearing. In fact, I felt my heart do a bit of an acrobatic leap. To disguise this traitorous reaction I took a large bite of Mrs. Cooper's potted beef and sat there chewing it thoroughly, a concentrated expression on my face. Sir John didn't even glance my way for a full two minutes, so I might as well not have bothered.

When he turned to me, a facile smile had taken the place of his more serious concern. "Shall we ride out at ten? Perhaps the two of us should have a bit of a talk about this matter—where we won't be overheard."

"Very well," I said primly. Though I wondered whether it was a good idea, I really could not resist the opportunity. Of course, I assumed I would learn more from him than he would from me.

My riding outfit is rather delightful, if I do say so myself. Mama had allowed me, against Amanda's expressed wishes, to purchase a steely shade of blue, finished up the front with braiding. There is a hint of that same color in my eyes, though they are green, and it makes them somehow more noticeable. On this occasion I chose to wear it because the day was warm, not because I was riding out with Sir John, of course.

It seemed to me that I should be the one to choose our destination, as I knew the area. But Sir John merely waited for me to mount before leading the way. Miffed, I said nothing, but allowed Lofty to follow Apollo down through the woods on the other side of the stables. Sir John turned to smile at me from time to time, but made no attempt to start a conversation. After a while I became aware that he was actually circling back in the direction of the estate. I instantly understood where he was leading and made a vigorous protest.

"I will not have this discussion by the pond," I said indignantly. "How could you think of such a thing?

Don't you understand that that was an embarrassing moment for me and not an occasion of which I care to be reminded?''

''Embarrassing?'' he called back, that devilish gleam in his eyes. ''Nothing could be further from my wishes than to see you embarrassed. I would far prefer that you were comfortable with the whole idea. It's warm enough today for both of us to have a little dip in your secret pond.''

''Don't be ludicrous! We will do no such thing.''

''Very well. But the pond is a good place for our talk, one where we can be sure no one is within hearing range.''

There was something so determined about his chin that I felt it would do me absolutely no good to argue with him. He had obviously visited the area since the day we met, for he had discovered a way to ride the horses around the small wood and leave them where they would not be discovered. When he came to assist me down from Lofty, he placed his hands firmly at my waist and lifted me down, retaining his grip for long seconds afterward.

''I am perfectly capable of standing by myself,'' I assured him, brushing away his hands. ''Follow me, then, and we can sit on the rocks in the sun.'' Right where he had sat that first day, actually. But there was nothing for it.

Sir John had removed his boots and carried them in one hand. His other hand was at my elbow, as though I needed his assistance to make my way over the rocks. He kept staring at my bare feet, as though they were some symbol of my depravity. His own feet were far stronger and more impressive than I would have suspected. Once through the narrow passage he moved in front of me and climbed up to where he had sat before.

''Too bad you haven't brought your throat-ripping

dog along this time," he murmured. "Such an impressive beast."

I could almost laugh with him, but not quite. Especially when I noticed that he was loosening his collar. "You are not going to remove your clothes," I said. "If you do, I shall leave here immediately."

"I have no intention of removing my clothes. Unless, of course, you wish to do so yourself, and then we could both swim without any hesitation."

Refusing to give this suggestion the least consideration, I sniffed and turned the conversation to a different topic. "I want you to tell me why you are up at night and nosing about the place. How did you discover the Masked Rider, and why did you follow him?"

"I have my share of curiosity, my dear girl. And it has been well whetted by the extraordinary events around Hastings."

"You'll have to do better than that. From the first you were spying about. Long before you saw any Masked Rider."

He considered me with those expressive dark eyes of his. "That was your imagination, remember? It was you who wandered about at night, trying to trap me with threads across my door and excursions to my bed."

I could tell, of course, that he was trying to enrage me. Unfortunately, he was succeeding rather well. The spleen rose within me to an alarming level and I could feel my cheeks redden with heat, my heart hammer in frustration. But Sir John wasn't finished.

"It seems most likely to me that it is you who has a secret to hide. That indeed it is you who masks herself and rides out at night, robbing people on the nearby roads of their possessions. What do you have to say to that, Catherine?"

•9•

It had never occurred to me that he thought it might be me whom he had followed. To be sure, I was only slightly shorter than Cousin Bret and only modestly taller than Mama or Amanda, but how could anyone for even a moment believe I was a high-wayman? I was so astonished and so insulted that I said only, "You can't possibly believe that."

"I'm not sure whether I believe it or not," he admitted. "It wouldn't be totally out of character for you. Only slightly more outrageous than your progress through London, your swimming naked in this pond, who knows what else."

For the briefest moment I almost wished that I was indeed that reckless, that fearless, though of course never that lawless. I thought of the freedom one would have to experience to behave in that fashion. Oh, I might have been wild for the likes of our country society, but not that wild.

". . . were you doing up?"

I seemed to have missed what he was saying. With an effort I brought my mind back to where I was, sitting in the sun on a hard rock, just gazing at him. "I beg your pardon?"

"Catherine, I want you to answer my questions seriously." His voice was warm and comforting. I think he must have believed that he could fool me into trusting him. "If you will just tell me what you know about

115

this business, I'm sure I can clear it up. You mustn't worry about any untoward consequences. I promise you that I will be discreet.''

That made me frown at him. ''Why should you be? And what business is this of yours?''

He sat there for a long time. At length he shrugged his broad shoulders and sighed. ''You don't need to know that, my dear.''

''Well, of course I do,'' I protested hotly. And then true inspiration hit me. ''Did Robert send you for this purpose?''

He hesitated for a moment and then nodded.

''But why? What does he know about what's been happening here?''

''Very little, I'm afraid. But he felt he needed to know more.''

''That's scarcely an answer at all.'' I shifted on the jagged rock, trying to find a reasonably comfortable position. ''What does Robert know? He hasn't been down here for months. Since way before the highwayman . . . Well, for months, at least. How could he have heard anything?''

''I believe your estate manager mentioned something in one of his reports. And then there is the earl, ever curious about this part of the countryside.'' At my look of horror, he hastened to add, ''Not that he suspects anything wrong at Hastings. He merely believes that your family should be in a position to put anything right that is wrong in the entire neighborhood.''

''He would.''

''Yes, I'm afraid so. And there was, of course, my own adventure with the highwayman.'' He regarded me with a certain curiosity, as though I might be some strange species of animal that he hadn't encountered before. ''Really, I think you would be wise to confide in me.''

The poor fellow actually harbored the suspicion that it was I who rode out in that outlandish costume. It would have been funny if the situation hadn't been so serious. Did I dare to tell him what little I knew? What if it was damning to someone when he put it together with whatever he had learned?

"Tell me what Robert commissioned you to do."

Sir John shrugged. "He merely wished for me to look into the matter, Catherine. He didn't feel that he could come down himself just now. And he was willing to let me choose a pair for him, so here I am."

"What is so difficult about his coming down here? Why does he insist on remaining in London?"

"I don't think there's any problem." His tone became soothing and gentle. "He simply doesn't wish to appear at Hastings for the time being."

It was while I was contemplating this circular reasoning that Sir John chose to distract me completely. He moved a little closer to me and began to run his fingers gently through the wisps of hair that always straggled over my ears. I could feel the texture of his fingertips on my ears and then wandering around to the back of my neck. I didn't know quite what he was doing, but I suspected that it wasn't proper, and I had no intention of stopping him.

His fingers wove a pattern on the back of my neck while he continued to regard me with luminous eyes, their message at once silent and intense. I could feel the depth of his desire to kiss me. Even his lips moved with the need. I pouted mine, in a provocative way but tentatively, and a small grin tugged at the corners of his mouth. "Do you want me to kiss you, Catherine?"

My head came up proudly. "Only if you haven't kissed Amanda."

Then he leaned toward me and my heart leapt in my chest as his lips brushed softly against mine. Oh, he

knew just what to do. One of the local boys, Gerald
Harkins, had thought he kissed with extraordinary
dexterity because he latched firmly on to my mouth.
If only the poor fellow had had some idea of real tech-
nique! The wispy touch Sir John bestowed on me left
me aching for more. My mouth burned with the desire
to feel real pressure, real passion from his embrace.
But his lips did not return.

Instead, they wandered off to my cheeks and my
nose and my hastily closed eyes. His touch was like
magic, evoking a warmth and excitement wherever it
landed. My heart started to beat faster, my insides to
churn in a most alarming manner. All of this before
his lips returned to mine, capturing them with a light
determination that made me consider why women were
rumored to swoon during such antics. If not swoon,
at least quite lose their heads. I felt as if I had lost
mine, certainly. If my life had depended upon it, I
don't think I could have drawn back from him.

His hands held me at the waist, pressing against me
so firmly that I almost felt as though there were no
material between his skin and mine. And then, his
hands moved slightly upward. My breathing became
shallow with alarm, or something quite like it. The
closer his hands moved to my breasts, the more
alarmed and hopeful I became. I wanted him to touch
me there so fiercely that I nearly said so. But his hands
stopped right beneath the swelling out of my Empire
gown, tucked under the blush of my femininity. I realized that he was not going to make a further move
that way.

He drew me against his chest then, and there was
some relief in that, because the pressure relieved the
ache the smallest bit. His lips never left mine, though,
and we remained in that position for a very long time,
his arms around me, crushing me against his chest. I
would not have minded if we had remained that way

all day. My disappointment was great when he at
length loosened his grip on me and set me a tiny way
apart from him.

"Will you tell me about these nighttime adventures
of yours?" he asked persuasively. "You can trust me,
Catherine."

I shifted slightly and smoothed down the skirt of my
riding costume, which had crept up almost to my
knees. It took me a moment to catch my breath. "I'm
not the one who dresses in that silly, melodramatic
costume. Wouldn't you have recognized my voice? The
highwayman must have spoken to you when you were
robbed."

"Yes, but the voice was disguised and came through
the cloth of the mask. It could have been yours."

"Well, it wasn't." But I said this in a manner lacking conviction. Why should I trust him? I still was not
sure how much I wanted him to know, or not know.
Weren't his kisses meant to enchant me so that I would
pour out my heart to him? Stubbornly, I felt that I
wanted him to be as confused as I was.

"It would be the adventure that attracts you," he
mused, half-convinced again that I was indeed the
highwayman. He ran a hand roughly through his thick
hair, frowning unhappily at me. "You really mustn't
do it. One of these days a gentleman is going to draw
his pistol and shoot you dead. You have to understand
that it is very annoying for a gentleman to be robbed
on the high road. He's not going to stop to ask himself
if you might possibly be a woman, or be out for the
sport of it. He's simply going to shoot you."

I felt a shiver run down my spine. "You exaggerate,
Sir John. Besides, I've told you it isn't I."

"Then perhaps we could work together to solve the
mystery," the baronet suggested.

Oh, I could see right through his ploy, but I pretended to go along with him. "Yes, indeed, we must

rid the neighborhood of this villain. You and I could take turns. It must be very tiring for you, staying up half the night and all the day.''

''I'm not complaining,'' he said, a curious light in his eyes. ''But I would certainly enjoy spending the nights on guard with you.''

I ignored his teasing. ''Then we will arrange for a watch this evening and perhaps find out the truth of the matter.''

''I doubt the villain rides out every single night.''

''Really? You think him a poor-spirited fellow who only gains the courage occasionally?''

''Not that, but he couldn't risk going out too often. Otherwise the local authorities would soon trap him . . . and execute him.''

As he'd expected, that word shocked me. Execution was, of course, what they did to captured and convicted highwaymen. The very thought of it made me sick to my stomach, and I hopped up from my seat on the uncomfortable rock. ''Perhaps you will devise a plan and let me know of it. I can't think of a thing right now.''

I stepped down to the pond, catching a reflection of my flushed face in the water. Whether it had become flushed when we kissed, or more recently from the thought of death, I could not say. In either case, I put my hands to my cheeks to cool them, hoping to regain my composure.

I saw Sir John reflected in the water, right behind me, regarding me with interest. ''I could take care of you,'' he said. ''I could make everything all right.''

''Everything *is* all right. You needn't concern yourself with me. I'm perfectly capable to taking care of myself.''

''I don't doubt it.'' He laid a hand intimately at the nape of my neck under my curling hair. ''Bear the dangers in mind. And the potential for the disgrace of your family.''

I shook his hand off my body. It was far too disturbing. ''You're warning the wrong person, my dear sir.''

''Ah, yes. I had forgotten.'' His eyes seemed larger than usual, and a frown creased his forehead. ''Think about it, Catherine. I would hate to see any harm come to you.''

''You needn't concern yourself.''

I left him standing there, staring absently into the pool. As I headed back toward the passage, carrying my boots in my hand, I called to him, ''Come along, Sir John. The horses will be impatient.''

My mother managed to avoid me for the rest of the day. Even when I cornered her just before dinner, she started to talk very absently, as if I were a maid rather than her daughter. I was not at all fooled by this behavior, of course, but I knew it meant she had no intention of confiding in me. And then, after dinner, Amanda pulled me out of the sitting room, where Sir John and Cousin Bret were bickering in a gentlemanly fashion over the price of a good horse. My sister was outraged with me over something, but I could not for the moment understand what it was.

''Your behavior is simply inexcusable,'' she ranted, wringing her soft white hands in a most ladylike semblance of distress. I decided that I would someday have to learn how to do that, just in case it managed to impress anyone. ''One would have thought you'd been brought up by a band of gypsies, for all the thoughtfulness you show.''

''If I knew to what you were referring,'' I replied, in my most reasonable tone, ''I would attempt to answer you, my dear sister. Pray enlighten me.''

''Oh, yes. How could you possibly, out of all your

misdeeds, remember the one in particular with which I have chosen to chastise you?''

Sometimes even Amanda shows a turn for sarcasm. She may have picked it up from Mama rather than me, but it adds something to her stature, in my eyes.

''You have been harassing Mama again and she's quite distressed with you. You know very well that she doesn't understand why you and I can't see her ghosts. What is the purpose in hounding her about them?''

''I haven't hounded Mama about anything that is not of the utmost importance. I wouldn't think of badgering her about her ghosts. Let her have them, and welcome, I say.''

''Now you know that isn't true! You were in her room this morning, and I saw her trying to shake you off just before dinner. Really, Catherine! I'm surprised at you.''

''I don't see why. You know how thoughtless I am. Did you not wish to scold me for riding out alone with Sir John this afternoon?'' I simply could not resist that, since I felt sure she wasn't aware of my having gone with him.

Amanda gave me a cool look and shook her head sadly. ''I know all about that. Sir John spoke to me as soon as he returned to the house. My advice would be to show a little less attention to him, sister. And indeed, he's not the sort of man to become attached to a sad romp.''

''Whyever would you think that?''

''Because he is a gentleman born and bred. He will wish to choose as a wife a woman who will be looked up to by his neighbors and friends. His estate in Wiltshire is the envy of the area for fifty miles around.''

''Well, if he told you that, there is something amiss with his modesty.''

She drew herself up with self-righteous poise. ''I assure you he told me nothing of the sort. I was able to glean the idea from a few remarks that he made, especially those about the vicar depending on a solid Christian influence from the wives of the gentry.''

Oh, I could picture him feeding her that pabulum. What a charlatan the man was! ''Well, never mind what he says. Sir John would do well to look for someone a little less virtuous, if I am not mistaken.''

''What do you mean by that?'' she demanded.

It seemed to me as good a time as any to begin to educate my sister on the subject of Sir John. ''I think perhaps he is not the model of modesty and virtue that you and Mama would make him out to be. If I'm not mistaken, he's quite a lady's man in London. But you needn't take my word for it. I've written to my friend Lady Sutton, and I'm sure she'll be able to tell us a little more about our visitor.''

''She will know nothing more than the gossip of the *ton*,'' Amanda informed me stiffly.

Mama appeared in the doorway and frowned at the two of us. ''What is this chatter in the hallway?'' she demanded almost petulantly. ''You have company in the sitting room, my dears. You might entertain the gentlemen with a game of cards.''

Amanda and I hastened after her, aware that we had ignored our guests in order to have a little sisterly feud. Sir John regarded us with interest. I could tell that he would question Amanda on our conference at the first possible moment. Cousin Bret, wearing that infatuated grin of his, had jumped to his feet to welcome my sister's return.

We managed to take our seats at the games table without any further disagreement, though I gathered that Cousin Bret had hoped to have Amanda as his partner rather than me. His comments, made in a rather high-pitched tone, went something like: ''What is this? I thought Amanda was to be my partner! Cousin Catherine is of all players the worst I have ever come across. She will not concentrate on the game. It's most unfair for me to have to partner her this evening, when she could very well be Sir John's partner.'' And so forth. But I paid no heed to him.

Sir John cocked his head at me, in a challenging manner, and declared himself ready to be the undoing of me. ''That is, unless you have an inclination to pay attention this evening, Miss Ryder. It doesn't sound likely, though, if your cousin is to be believed.''

''One should never believe my cousin without sufficient reason,'' I retorted. Cousin Bret didn't even kick me under the table for this aspersion on him, because he was already engaged in arranging his cards.

Mama floated about the room. When first I saw that she meant to wander, I was slightly alarmed that she would also begin to ramble. One of her talks with ghosts simply would not do in front of Cousin Bret.

Sir John was rather handy at cards as a rule, but we chose to play a game he hadn't set his mind to since he was a child. He immediately got into the spirit of the lottery tickets round game, though, and staked his counters with great enthusiasm. It was rather charming to see him so delighted with our fun.

Cousin Bret grumbled about the childishness of the game and eventually we were forced to switch to whist. Not that that satisfied him. He insisted that I wasn't concentrating, but he was actually to blame for the biggest fiasco. He had somehow managed to misplace one of his cards; it stuck to the back of another one, and it threw his calculations completely off. When this mistake was discovered he treated us to a rare display of temper.

Throwing the cards down on the green baize, he narrowly missed knocking over his port glass. ''I might have known!'' he trumpeted. ''Sticky cards. I can't remember when I have played with such old, sticky cards. At the clubs in London they bring out a new pack practically hourly. But not here! Oh, no! Not at Hastings! It would be entirely too modern and normal for you, no doubt.''

All of this was directed at me, but Mama stood off to the side, observing her nephew as though he were some kind of odd creature from the wilds. It would never have occurred to her to bring out a new deck of cards. I daresay we had half a dozen of them, but the three of us, when we are playing alone, have a great love of soft, familiar cards, sticky though they may be in humid weather.

''You really are a spoilsport,'' I informed him. ''If you want to play with brand-new cards, perhaps you should go to London.''

Amanda would have liked to scold me for this outburst, but she was seriously annoyed with Cousin Bret herself. She leapt to her feet and hastened over to Mama, putting an arm protectively around her. But Mama was not offended by Cousin Bret. He had merely set off a train of thought that she voiced without realizing that she spoke aloud.

''He was like that as a child,'' she mused. ''I remember when he broke the pony cart and blamed it on Robert. When he knew very well that I had seen what happened.''

Cousin Bret, cheeks flushed with angry red spots, pushed back his chair and rose. ''I fear your memory is not quite accurate, my dear Mrs. Ryder. However, it is no matter. If you all will excuse me, I have letters to write. Good night!''

Mama smiled graciously at him, still unaware that he had heard her. Sir John maintained a stoical expression, while Amanda and I exchanged covert glances. I suppose it seemed best to all of us to let the subject drop. Mama seated herself at Cousin Bret's place and took over his part in the game. It was delightful to see how much she enjoyed herself, and the thought occurred to me that it was not possible that either Amanda or Mama could possibly be the highwayman.

Which left Cousin Bret. And somehow I found it even more difficult to believe it of him after this evening's episode. Spoiled, a bad sport, petulant, argumentative. He was all those things. But surely he didn't have the wits and courage to brave the high road.

By the end of the evening I was more confused than ever, and exhausted with the effort of preserving the appearance of good-natured normality. As I trudged wearily up to my room, I realized that the baronet and I had not agreed on any plan to waylay the masked figure, that night or any other. But I was far too discouraged and bone-weary to care.

Instead of attempting to speak with Sir John, I went to my room, changed into my nightclothes, and climbed into bed. Sometime in the depth of the night I dreamed that he came into my room, carrying a candle, dressed for riding. He stood there by the door, gazing across the room at me. I was propped up against mountains of pillows, in a flimsy, gauzy gown that you could see right through, but I was far from embarrassed about the way his eyes lingered on my figure.

It occurred to me then that we were about to behave in a most unseemly fashion, which I anticipated with pounding heart and racing pulse. In my dream this was something that had happened before, but at some level I could feel the expectation of learning a tremendous secret, breathlessly, anxiously, eagerly being taken into the mysteries of that man and woman bond that I had heard referred to as ''conjugal bliss.''

Suddenly the dream fled, vanished like a wisp of thought, and I was devastated. My body ached with unsatisfied longings in that dark, warm room. My mind refused to accept the reality of my being alone, curled up under the fragrant sheet. Try as I might, I could not call the dream back.

I was so disturbed by not learning the promised secrets that I scarcely considered what might have interrupted my sleep. And I did not wish to consider what had inspired the dream.

·10·

The next day there was a letter from my friend Lady Sutton. I took it from Williams, called to Dutch to accompany me, and wandered out into the morning sunlight to read it. Dutch was in one of his rare playful moods and refused to let me concentrate on the three-page missive. First he tugged at my shoe-laces and then he insisted on putting his stubby paws on my knees, the farthest he could reach.

"Go away, you pesky dog," I admonished him. But he would have none of it. With baleful eyes he began a mournful groan that sounded much like a cow in pain. "Now stop that!"

"He merely wants your attention," a familiar voice informed me.

Sir John was dressed for riding, as he had been in my dream the previous evening, and I was hard-pressed not to blush. The rest of my body, too, had a decided response to his presence, which I vainly attempted to ignore. "Why don't *you* pay some attention to him?" I suggested.

His eyes crinkled with mirth. "This throat-ripping hound? I wouldn't dare get within ten feet of the brute."

Nonetheless, he picked up a stick and threw it for Dutch. Now Dutch is not really a retriever type of dog, but he was taken with the baronet and dutifully loped over to where the stick had fallen. Rather than pick it up, he stood guard over it until Sir John in frustration called him back.

"Just what is this animal capable of doing?" he inquired.

"Not much, but he's the most loyal beast in nature." I gave a little shake to the letter I held, eyeing him carefully as I said, "Now, if you want to know what an animal is capable of, let me just read you a part of this letter I've received."

My threat held about as much influence as the original one concerning Dutch. Sir John gave me a look of mock horror and settled himself on the stone bench beside me, making much of disposing himself comfortably and turning to hear me with an expression of polite concentration. I would like to have kicked him in the shin.

"This is what my friend Bethany has written with regard to your character."

Oh, he shuddered with feigned alarm and I only wished that Bethany had been even more to the point. I was sure she could have been.

" 'My dear Catherine, It was so delightful to hear from you. I feared you had quite forgotten me and our delicious adventures during your Season. I still laugh when I think what some poor gentleman is missing by not having won you then.' " I thought Sir John gave a snort of mirth at this point, but when I glanced over at him, he was sitting stiff as a statue, listening intently. " 'Martin sends his dearest love. I half-suspect that he would have offered for you himself had I not been making eyes to distract him!' She's only teasing, of course," I explained to Sir John.

"Of course."

" 'Now, as to Sir John Meddows, I was astonished to hear that he had made himself at home at Hastings when your brother Robert is in town. Sir John and Robert are, as you must know, the very best of friends.

But Robert feels an obligation to the Earl of Stonebridge, which tends to keep his behavior in line, while Sir John has absolutely no check on his. My dear, you would not believe the tales about him. If even a third of them are true, he is the most astonishing rake.

" 'Not that he's ever been accused of mistreating his women, but there have been so many of them! You will understand, from being acquainted with his dark good looks, that he has attracted half of the unattached young ladies, but his preference seems to be for married or not so respectable ones! Honestly, I believe I know half a dozen women who would not scorn a small tête-à-tête with him. Not including myself, of course!' "

"Oh, drat!" he muttered. "And here I was planning to seduce her when I returned to town."

There was a great deal of laughter in his voice, but I paid no heed to it. I had already realized that I shouldn't have read the whole of Bethany's letter to him, but it was too late by then. At least he would understand exactly what I had learned of his true character.

"To continue," I said, in a monstrously cool tone of voice. " 'He is rumored to have some interest in Marguerite Larson, and to have had a short term affair with Molly Winslow, but neither of them has ever said a word. So perhaps it is all fantasy. Except! I did myself see him once leaving the home of a rather questionable woman at seven o'clock in the morning. Do not ask me what I was doing up at that hour, for it is not half so interesting as it sounds. My dearest husband is planning to . . .' Well, that is all she has to say about you."

He considered the gossip with Olympian calm. "There are always tales about unattached men, Catherine. I'm not saying that I haven't done my share of courting of the ladies, but I've never harmed anyone."

I humphed at him. "So you say. Well, this is not the sort of record my sister would wish to hear, and I very much fear that she should be apprised of it."

He considered this with impartial detachment. "She won't like the fact that it's gossip, of course, but she'll be inclined to believe the account of a woman as well-placed and sensible as Lady Sutton. It will certainly shatter her illusions about me."

"Don't you care?"

His black Hessians gleamed in the sunlight and a breeze played with his thick, dark hair. Never had he seemed so uninterested and inaccessible as he did then. He might have been one of the London blades musing on the Season's collection of maidens. An arrogance that I hadn't witnessed before clung to him like a glove. When he spoke, it was with a voice quite different than his usual one. This one drawled in a lazy, offensive manner.

"I shouldn't want her to hate me, of course. That would be most distressing." He sounded suddenly just like all the men I had met in London, and I wanted to run away from him. But he kept me there with a stern look from those intense eyes. "Now your mother is a different matter. I shouldn't like it at all if she were ill disposed toward me. But I think, yes, I feel quite sure, that this report will not damage me in her eyes."

"No," I admitted, miffed beyond bearing. "Mama hasn't a prudish bone in her body."

"Still, I would suggest that you withhold the letter for a few days. Until everything is settled."

"What is there to be settled?" I asked him sharply.

"This highwayman business, for one thing. I think I really must make a concerted effort to apprehend the fellow, so that no rumors can find their way back to London. Your brother would expect as much of me."

If he had spoken of our working together to discover who the highwayman was, I would have felt a little better toward him. As he didn't, I rose abruptly and gave my skirts a dismissive shake. "Well, that has nothing to do with the letter. I cannot promise you that I won't show it to anyone. That is a matter on which I will have to make up my own mind."

He had hastened to his feet and now bowed smartly. "As you wish, of course, Miss Ryder. I'm sure you know how best to handle your own family."

Not that he believed it for a minute. It was just one more of his fancy phrases, part of the imitation he was enacting of a Bond Street beau. How I hated it! But it struck me that it was the role he'd played with Amanda all along. I couldn't imagine why he thought it would do anything other than repel *me*.

If Amanda hadn't pestered me the next morning about not doing my share of the chores, I probably would not have been so blunt with her. But I had continued to oversee exactly those who had always been in my care: the dairy maids, the laundry maids, the stable boys, and every other outdoor employee at Hastings. Her duties seemed much simpler to me, and tidier, just directing the indoor staff.

"You will never learn to manage a household if you continue to skulk about in this fashion," Amanda informed me. "Mama has told you that you are to help me choose the menu. You won't have the slightest idea how to go on if you ever marry."

Mama had mentioned that I might, if I wished, ask the cook for dishes I particularly liked. She had never suggested that I share the duty of choosing meals with Amanda.

But I could see what it was. Amanda thought that Sir John was paying more attention to me now and she was afraid that he meant to ask me to marry him. Which made her very cross. I thought it was as good a time as any to disillusion her as to his character.

"If you must make such an untrue statement, I wish you would not link it with the idea of marriage," I protested. "You aren't to be thinking that Sir John Meddows means to make either of us an offer. No such thing! I've long suspected he had a most deplorable reputation, and my dear friend Bethany confirms it in her letter."

"You have solicited gossip from Lady Sutton!" How indignant she was, trying to hide her curiosity. "You know it is wrong to gossip about people. How could you listen to slanderous tales of Sir John? Why, he's your own brother's very best friend."

"I daresay it doesn't bother Robert one bit that Sir John is a rake. In fact, it probably brings him into contact with just the sort of women he wishes to know at this time of his life."

"Catherine! I'm ashamed to hear you speak in such a fashion. And I never, ever considered that Sir John would make either of us an offer. And I'm sure your friend Lady Sutton is quite mistaken on this head."

"Not a bit of it," I assured her cheerfully. "Shall I get the letter and read it to you?"

From the flash of anger in her eyes I could tell that she was remarkably cross with me. Amanda was far too principled to contemplate slapping me for my insolence, but she was likely to run to Mama with tales of my misdeeds, so I suggested a compromise. "Mama, of course, need know nothing of this. She's determined to be charmed by Sir John, and his presence seems to calm her."

That brought her around a little. She sniffed delicately. "Except for the night when she would speak with Papa. Did Sir John ever mention that occasion to you?"

"I don't think so, directly. He probably thought very little of it. He's a most tolerant man, you know."

"Obviously. I would never dream of upsetting

Mama. If she's attached to the baronet, it may distract her from her grief.''

I only wish it had. "She would be more distracted if he carried one of us off and married us, but Bethany's letter suggests that it is the dalliance and not the sticking point that is his specialty.''

Since she seemed receptive enough by then to hear the whole, I explained what my friend had said. Amanda's lips twitched with disapproval and her eyes narrowed as she said, ''Not at all the sort of man he has passed himself off to be. Whatever can be the point of his playing such a game?''

But I didn't want her to know about all the other untoward things that were going forward. She was likely to have a fit of the vapors or burst into floods of tears. When Amanda didn't know what to do about a situation, she cried. Not a very useful substitute for action.

''He's only come to look out a pair of horses for himself, and one for Robert, and I daresay he doesn't know how to behave himself other than to make himself pleasing to whatever ladies he finds available.'' This just slipped out of my mouth, but the more I thought about it, the more I became convinced that it was true. And the more melancholy I felt.

Amanda sighed and clasped her soft white hands together. ''Well, it won't do any harm to have him around for our Public Day. He's just the sort of man who could make the whole occasion a huge success— dance with all the girls, talk about sporting events with the other gentlemen, and make the servants feel most comfortable in their entertainments. Charming men are so very useful. It's such a pity they aren't honorable.''

Such cynicism was unlike Amanda and I worried about her. But only for a moment. Then Sir John appeared at the door of the summer parlor, where we were sitting, a broad smile on his face and a devilish gleam in his eyes.

"I wonder if I might join the two most delightful young ladies in the country," he said. His gaze was full upon Amanda, an intent, knowing expression on his face. I felt quite sure he must have overheard a good bit of our conversation.

Amanda lost her composure. Her hands fluttered about at her waist almost as if they had a life of their own. "Oh, I don't . . . Uhm, you mustn't . . . Really, I should go to see Mama on the instant. She will wonder where I have gotten, and scold me for being so long about the linens." She gave the briefest of nods to Sir John before fleeing on her little slippered feet at a pace one could only describe as a run.

"Now, what could possibly have taken possession of your sister?" He turned his knowing, intent expression on me, hoping, no doubt, to throw me into disorder as well. At the same time he continued into the room, walking right up to me.

"You know very well what has happened. I have been forced to enlighten her as to your wicked reputation."

"Wicked?" He took a step closer to me, moving with that uncanny grace that made my hands tremble. "Don't you mean passionate? Or perhaps dangerous? Don't you find me a little bit dangerous, Catherine?"

His silky voice was not meant to threaten me, but to remind me of how very enchanting he could be. Though I tried to resist the pull of his voice and his eyes and his nearness, I could not so much as back away from him. "N-no," I insisted bravely. "I don't find you dangerous, Sir John."

He caught hold of my trembling hands and brought them to his lips. It was no use pretending that he had no effect on me. His mouth brushed the skin on the back of my hands, and my fingers tightened over his.

"Aren't you tempted to run away from me, as your sister did?"

I had begun to feel reckless. "Not at all. I'm perfectly capable of restraining your ardor and making you behave yourself."

"I can't think why you would believe that." His grin was meant to entirely destroy me, which it very nearly did. Only by remembering where we were, and that a servant or even my mother could appear at any moment was I able to tug my fingers from his grip.

The gleam in his eyes alarmed me. I very much feared that he intended to kiss me right there. With a little skip backward I put myself momentarily out of his reach. "You wouldn't dare kiss me in such a public place."

"Rakes aren't concerned with such things, you know. We have only a burning desire to have our way with innocent young ladies. A true rake would no doubt ravish you right here on the Axminster carpet."

He was teasing me, of course, but that special light had appeared in his eyes, and I did wonder if he mightn't kiss me. Not that I would have minded, save for someone seeing us. That possibility was too great; I had yet to sink to such folly. With a stern look I strode to the door, informing him grandly, "You will do nothing of the sort. If there is ever anything of that nature forced upon me, I shall have my brother challenge you to a duel."

"There's not much of that going on anymore."

"I don't care," I cried. "I shall have him put a bullet through your heart."

He shook his head with wounded astonishment. "Would you do that? How very uncomfortable I should be. Do you, by any chance, know whether Robert is a decent shot?"

Far be it from me to admit that my brother could do little with a pistol, though he was fairly accurate with his birding gun. "Never mind that. My reputation would be protected."

He considered this with wry skepticism. "Nothing about a duel protects a lady's reputation. In fact, that reality couldn't be farther from the truth. A duel merely causes everyone to talk about her and wonder what she did to lead some poor fellow on."

No doubt he was right, but I wasn't going to listen to any more of his roguish chatter. It was meant merely to intrigue me. And I had no intention of being intrigued by the rascal. I gave one more huff, with my nose elevated to its most exalted height, and stalked from the room. As the door closed behind me, I could hear him laughing delightedly. The fact that he didn't follow me was cold comfort.

I returned to my room and slumped on my bed, intent on having a good session with myself about what was happening to my heart and my senses. Sir John seemed to have invaded both of them, drat the man. He had come from nowhere, gotten me stirred up, and might disappear at any time. He could even slip away back to London before the Public Day Mama was planning.

And I didn't know what condition I'd be in when he left. Something told me that I'd gotten far too attached to him in this short space of time. But I told myself, quite firmly, that it was nothing of the sort. Merely one of those sensual attractions that one read hints of in the more lurid novels of featherbrained young ladies such as Amanda, who was forever begging me to listen to just this one passage that I would surely swoon over. Yet here I was about to swoon over Sir John, who had done no more, according to his lights, than flirt with me when none of the rest of the family was around.

Well, I would just have to rid myself of this nonsensical attraction to Sir John. All it would take was resolution on my part. To clear my head and rid myself of some of my spleen, I slipped down the back stairs and headed for the stable. Lofty seemed to sense my disposition and we fairly flew down the trail that led to the spring. This was as far away from the pond as I could get. No use dredging up all those uncomfortable memories.

There was the dull murmur of summer insects and a very light breeze coming across the afternoon fields. I let Lofty have her head and I clung to her like a burr. You can only do that in the country, let loose that way. In London, even in Hyde Park, you had to ride at a very modest pace, never galloping at all. Even here, when I was younger, someone had always accompanied me. But I had shrugged off that restriction years ago.

When we reached the spring I dismounted to stand in the tall grasses and allow her a chance to lap at the cool, fresh water. I suppose I was daydreaming, for my mind certainly wasn't on any specific thought when I glanced up and saw Sir John, astride Thunder, watching me with an almost dumbstruck expression on his countenance. And there wasn't the least sign of arrogance or condescension to him in that moment.

Goosebumps sprang up on my arms, and I ducked my head to avoid the intensity of his gaze. There was nothing frightening about him; it wasn't that. He simply made me feel as if I were the only person who existed in the world, and I was unexpectedly overcome by shyness. Then, quite suddenly, he swung Thunder about and galloped off.

He was good on Thunder. Robert would have appreciated his skill; I was moved by his grace and power. But the moment he was out of sight, I began to doubt my own eyes. He hadn't spoken or in any way acknowledged my presence, and I began to think that he had been a figment of my imagination. That sort of thing could happen, if you rode out in the heat without your bonnet, as I had done. The gurgling of the spring, the cozy warmth of the sunlight . . .

I felt more confused than ever and sat down on a tussock of grass to consider what was happening to me. Though I stayed there for some time, until Lofty nudged me to get my attention, I reached no conclusions. When I arrived at the stable, Thunder was not in his stall and Sir John was nowhere about.

I happened to encounter Cousin Bret in the hallway. He was in a decidedly bad temper.

"Who gave Sir John permission to ride Thunder?" he demanded without preamble. "This is the second time in three days that he's taken Thunder out."

"Why shouldn't he ride Thunder?" I asked. "Sir John is a superior horseman and a great friend of Robert's. Of course he has our permission to take out Thunder."

Cousin Bret gave a grunt of annoyance and tugged angrily at the sleeves of his tight-fitting blue superfine coat. "It's very inconsiderate of you to offer him that privilege when you know Thunder is my choice of your stables."

"You're both guests at Hastings and I can't see why one of you should have exclusive access to Thunder. He's a difficult horse to manage, but Sir John has more than sufficient skill to exercise him properly." I considered this a diplomatic way of putting it; I could have told Cousin Bret that we found him only marginally able to control the horse.

He frowned prodigiously. "I think you overestimate Sir John's skills. He would do well to leave Thunder to me. Especially as I might wish to ride him late in the day and would want him fresh."

"Where would you ride him late in the day?" I asked, wondering if he would make such a request if it was to go highway-robbing that he had in mind.

His shoulders lifted in a negligent shrug. "To visit my friends in Cambridge. To go for a ride. No special reason."

"I hope you don't ride him off the road. Robert would be devastated if Thunder injured himself in any way."

"I'm sure you needn't worry about my riding."

His smug voice and condescending air may not have been calculated to raise my ire. Or they may have. "But I do, every time you ride him," I snapped.

Cousin Bret was impervious to my snubs. He laughed and walked away from me without further ado. Oh, how I hoped it turned out to be he who was our highwayman!

·11·

It took me a long time to discover where Mama was. Not that there was anything particularly odd about her being in the attics. She was wont to disappear among the treasures of her youth on occasion, and one would find her putting on the bonnets she had worn as a bride and a new wife, posing in front of the mirror.

And talking to my father, sometimes. Repeating conversations they'd once had, or reinventing the pleasures of their courting days. She looked young and pretty then, almost as if she'd transported herself back in time. That day she was seated on an old chair whose stuffing was leaking onto the floor, and a wonderful hat, loaded down like a basket of garden vegetables, sat in her lap.

"Isn't it wonderful?" she asked, motioning to the confection. "It was my very favorite, I think. Not Harold's, I fear. He never liked the ones with so much on them. Really, they were terribly heavy and rather hazardous, with their projecting spikes and feathers. One had to take special care. They used to make the most amazing likenesses of flowers and fruits and leafy things. A goat would have thought it the most wonderful concoction."

This was the hat she'd worn to have her portrait painted. Sometimes I think she forgot that. But it was in the gallery, the last in a long line of women married into the Ryder family, and she was probably the most striking of the women for the last hundred years. Even in the painting you could catch the hint of her whimsical nature and her otherworldliness. My father had adored the portrait.

"It's a wonderful hat. But I'm not surprised they went out of fashion."

It occurred to me that this might be the place where the black cape and mask had come from for the highwayman's costume. Everyone at Hastings knew about the trunks of old clothes. We'd used them on many occasions for dressing up, and for costume parties and local masquerades. I began to dig through the layers of silks and satins and superfine coats, looking for some clue to this mystery.

"What are you trying to find?" Mama asked. The hat had shifted to one side of her head and she looked almost like an actress dressed for a farce on stage. My fingers went instantly to straighten it, to bring back my own Mama. There was something too unsettling about her playing a role.

"I thought we had an old black cloak. Wasn't it in this trunk? The one Papa wore when he had to ride to his mother's in the rain?"

Did I imagine it, or was there something evasive about her glance, then? "I doubt if it would have been good enough to keep, after all those years of hard use." She quickly lifted the bonnet from her head and placed it in the open hatbox at the foot of her chair, along with some others. "Do you think we could make over one of these smaller ones for Amanda? This is such a pretty color, don't you think?"

If she was hoping to distract me, she was wide of the mark. I've never been interested in clothes above half, especially not Amanda's clothes. "You should ask Amanda. I'm not fond of that color, myself. It looks to soft and girlish. But about the cloak, Mama.

I'm sure I've seen it in one of the trunks. Perhaps in the larger in the corner.''

"No, I'm sure it's not here." She was very firm about this. Much more firm than Mama usually was about anything. "It was thrown away years ago. You remember it from when you were a child, in the years after Harold's mother died.''

I could be firm myself. "No. It's been within the last year or two that I saw it. And I doubt if one of the servants would have discarded it without asking permission. So where do you suppose it can have gotten to, Mama?''

"Oh, I don't know." She fluttered her hands dismissively. "It's not important. It wasn't at all a valuable item.''

Definitely there was something amiss with her reaction. Anything that had belonged to my father was almost sacred to her since his death. Unless she was hiding something, she would not behave in this offhand manner. I could feel a hard knot of fear forming in my stomach. I'm not sure that anything I have ever said, before or since, was as difficult as what I said then.

"You know, Mama, that cape could easily be the one the Masked Rider was wearing when I saw him leave the house the other night. Saw him . . . or her.''

She pretended not to hear me. Her hands were folded in her lap and her head rested back against the chair, with wisps of graying brown hair straggling down on her neck. She looked nothing at all like a highwayman.

"Did you know that Sir John had been robbed by a highwayman on the Newmarket Road a month ago?'' I asked, pressing her hard.

"Sir John?" Her eyes remained closed, but she found it difficult to ignore this bit of information. "Was he robbed of anything valuable?''

"Enough. Mama, I'm almost sure he has come down here to discover who is to blame."

Her eyes blinked open. A frown settled deep on her forehead. "I think you must be mistaken, my dear. He's a friend of Robert's and he has come here to choose a pair of horses for himself and your brother."

"That's just his excuse," I parried. "He has every intention of discovering the identity of the highwayman. And he thinks the highwayman comes from this house. In fact, occasionally he seems to think that I am the highwayman."

How she laughed. I hadn't heard her so amused in over a year. "Oh, my dear, he is quizzing you. Don't pay the least attention. You, a highwayman!" And she went off into gales of laughter.

"Mama, he has every reason to wish to bring the perpetrator to justice. He lost over fifty guineas."

"A mere bagatelle to a gentleman of his circumstances, I should think. He's probably only curious. Do you think Robert will come down for the Public Day?"

Her change in direction startled me. "I haven't the slightest idea. Mama, what are we to do about Sir John's suspicions?"

"Not take the least notice of them. They are patently ridiculous." The line of her mouth tightened. "Does this mean that he has no interest in you or Amanda? How sad. And how very cruel of him to toy with your affections. I think I shall ask him to leave."

"You can't do that."

"Whyever not? I asked him to stay, and now I will ask him to leave."

It was not as simple as that, and Mama knew it, but I could tell that she was upset. Whether this was because Sir John might be about to unearth the highwayman, or because her daughters were being treated shabbily by a gentleman of the *ton*, I could not fathom.

"Please don't ask him to leave. Perhaps he does have some interest in one of us."

Her lips softened and she patted my hand. "I see. Well, don't get your hopes up, my child. I have the tiniest bit of suspicion that Sir John may be what we used to call a lady's man. Not that I mean to cast any doubt upon his integrity. There are simply some men who cannot seem to choose from among the fairer sex, and spend all their time flitting from one to another."

She rose from her chair and gazed off into the distance. One hand moved up to pat her hair into place, as the hat had mussed it considerably. "A charming man, to be sure. So very handsome, don't you think?"

I agreed that Sir John was handsome. I agreed that he was charming. "But he's also devilishly frustrating and distressing," I muttered.

I don't know whether she heard me. "Do be a good girl and put that reticule back in the trunk for me, will you? Wrap it carefully in the cloth so that it won't get dusty. I'm really so pleased that it's managed to stay in such good shape for so many years. Do you think we could make the entertainment on Public Day a dress party so that I might carry it again?"

From then on I was unable to divert her attention from Public Day. She would talk about costumes, and the chances of Robert appearing on our doorstep, and whether Sir John was the type of man who would enjoy a masquerade. Just before we left the attics she smiled and said, "Don't worry about it, dear. Everything will work out just fine."

But I was not sure to what she referred, and I was too exhausted to try to find out. "Come, Mama, it's time to dress for dinner."

I let her descend the stairs while I remained behind to place the reticule carefully in the trunk with the old gowns and parasols and all the paraphernalia of Mama's Season in London. It had only taken her one Season to find herself a husband.

I couldn't help but wonder if things would have been different if I had met Sir John during my Season. Would he have seen that I was different from the other girls? Was I? And was he really different than all those regimented men I had met—caught up in that artificial world, depending on it for the meaning in their lives? He would probably never have noticed me at all.

No, I didn't believe that, really. Both of us were different. We would have noticed each other. But nothing might have come of it. Just being different wasn't everything. It didn't mean that we belonged together or that we were alike in the right kinds of ways. I was not naïve about his past, nor about my own shortcomings as a wife for a baronet.

With a sigh I followed Mama down the stairs. How did it always happen that I ended up thinking about Sir John instead of solving this matter of the Masked Rider?

From that moment on, Mama began feverishly making plans for the Public Day celebrations. We would have a small ball in the house after a day's entertainment out on the grounds. There was to be dining al fresco at midday with shuttlecock and other games afterward. I longed to see how good Sir John would prove to be at a local exhibition of cricket. He had regaled Amanda with tales of his expertise, when he was trying to impress her, and now we would have an opportunity to see if this was mere braggadocio.

For myself, there were a million tasks I had to accomplish. We would be using the grounds for special activities and they had to be groomed especially carefully. The servants were all excited about the big day, because of course it was a special time for them as well. In our family it was a tradition to reward them with special gifts for their excellent help.

Amanda and I were the ones who chose the presents, and it was a complex task. Mama had once insisted that they would prefer money to the actual gift, and though that might have been true, the one time Papa tried it, he found that they were insulted because we had not gone to our usual trouble of selecting just the right thing.

So Amanda and I went around to the families on our regular visits, noting whether this cottage had curtains, and whether that frying pan was beginning to develop rust holes. We kept careful records of this sort of thing, and the ages of the children, and enlisted Mr. Marks, the local mercantile king, in our efforts to choose appropriate treats.

Sir John was fascinated by this tradition and dogged our footsteps, making helpful remarks such as, "Now, why did you put down that they needed a new set of curtains when there was a definite lack of bootblacking in their home?" Such teasing comments called for smart rejoinders from me, while Amanda looked puzzled and tried to explain to him that the cottagers often lacked such necessities as bootblacking, but did not really consider them of the same importance that we did.

Sir John would smile at her and nod, but it was really to me that he spoke. The bond between us seemed to grow with his teasing and my replies. He seemed to enjoy it as much as I. I did notice, though, that there were times when he would question my sister on a particular point, under the guise of establishing gifts for the servants.

"Would you say that the Edmondses were a particularly needy family?" he asked after we had left their threadbare but clean cottage.

"Oh, yes. Mrs. Edmonds has been very sick over

the last year, since the baby was born.'' Amanda spoke with great earnestness. ''Mama thought at one point that Mrs. Edmonds was going to die. Jed is ever so grateful to her for her ministrations. He thinks Mama saved her life.''

What I got at this point was a thoughtful look from him. If it was Mama to whom Jed was grateful, that look seemed to say, would he be allowing me to ride out and waylay rich neighbors in the dark of night? Wouldn't he have informed Mama so that she could have stopped me? I had to be particularly devious to keep him from deciding that he had been wrong in his assessment.

''But you know Jed would give his loyalty to any of us,'' I scolded Amanda, as though she had slandered him by only noting Mama's influence. ''When Papa was alive, he once saved Jed's own life, years ago.''

''I don't remember that.'' Amanda's sweet little brow furrowed and she cocked her head at me. ''Papa was so modest. He never told me that tale at all. Did you witness the occasion?''

Because Sir John did not look convinced, I admitted that I had indeed done so. I may have gone too far in saying that Robert had as well, but it seemed a nice embellishment at the time.

''Thunder's sire was only newly acquired at the time. No one was any good at restraining him, but Jed was determined to please Papa by trying to train him. Robert and I had come up to the stables one evening when there was a bit of an uproar in the house. I think we had broken a vase or destroyed a flower bed. Some such thing. In any case, we found Jed up on the horse's back, with a very short rein and a very big problem. Oh, Lightning was bucking and stomping and doing everything he could to unseat the lad. You have to understand that even though Jed is small, he has absolutely no fear of horses, no matter how dangerous they are.''

"And how dangerous was this one?'' Sir John asked. He was leaning back against a tree where we had stopped to cool ourselves from the hot sun. There was a note of irony to his tone, which Amanda did not seem to recognize. I pretended I didn't, either.

"Oh, very. Just as Papa came striding up the path, Lightning threw Jed and broke loose, kicking out at him as he lay on the ground. Papa gave no thought to the danger at all. He charged into the stableyard and struck the horse away from Jed, heedless of the flying hooves.'' It was easy enough to describe the incident, since I had seen it happen, though not at Hastings and not to anyone I knew.

"How very dramatic.'' Sir John was bland and unimpressed. "No wonder Jed is grateful to all of you Ryders. He'd probably lie and cheat and steal for you without the least hesitation.''

Amanda was horrified at this interpretation of my story. "Oh, no, no! Jed is not that sort of fellow at all. He would of course be grateful to Papa, but he's an honest lad. Believe me, you are quite mistaken.''

"If you say so. I didn't mean to disparage the fellow's honesty,'' Sir John explained. "I merely wished to indicate that I understood his incredible obligation to your family—saving both his life and his wife's. That's quite a coincidence, when you think about it.''

"Not at all. It could happen to anyone,'' I assured him. Ready to leave the shade and perhaps even the presence of his searching eyes, I backed away from the tree and linked my arm with Amanda's. "Let's see if we can't find some fruit to take in to Mrs. Cooper, why don't we? She'd be delighted not to have to send one of the girls.''

Sir John laughed, but we ignored him.

* * *

Right after supper I excused myself and went out to the stables. It seemed to me that someone there had to be involved in whatever was going on. Whoever the Masked Rider was, surely he used a horse from our stables. And someone in the stables had to know about it.

What had begun to worry me was that I knew all the stable hands and I would have sworn that simple loyalty to our family would have prevented any of them from allowing a stranger, or even Cousin Bret, to ride out in the middle of the night in black cape and mask. Such folly, such danger, would not be permitted.

My Lofty was delighted to see me, but I passed her by with an absent pat and moved on to Antelope. It was Antelope who had gone missing for several days, and there had been several suspicious aspects to her return. She had looked very well-cared-for, for an animal that had run wild for the better part of a week. And she had a very slight tendency to favor her right foreleg, something I'd never seen in her before. Just as though she'd suffered a sprain and was almost, but not quite, as good as new.

I found Jed in the tack room, polishing brass and looking melancholy. His wife had been doing poorly since their baby was born six months before, and I asked after her.

"Ellen's not so well. Don't care so much for the food these days, ya see. If she don't eat, she'll just fade away to nothing and the babe with her."

"Has she been sent some of Mrs. Cooper's special broth?"

"That she has. Your mother seen to it. And for a while it worked. Now even that won't tempt her. Seems her stomach is too queer to take anything at all. Scares me, it does."

"Well, of course it does. Let me think about it. Perhaps I can find something that will agree with her.

I'll talk it over with Mr. Moore.'' Our local pharmacist was forever concocting herbal brews of intrinsically wretched taste, which somehow served their purpose on the odd occasion. "I may be riding out later," I said, very casually. "Will you be up late?"

"Now, what for would you be doing riding out at night?" His face crumpled up into a tight mask of concern. "You know better than to take that sweet mare out in the dark when she's not accustomed."

"Her night vision is a great deal better than mine. There's an errand I need to run."

"Best let me handle it. That's what I'm here for." He wouldn't meet my eyes.

"Now Antelope's night vision isn't as good, is it?"

"I wouldn't rightly know, miss."

"I imagine if Antelope were taken out at night she might take a tumble, might injure herself. But since she wasn't supposed to be out at night, how could she appear in the morning with an injury?"

Jed polished the brass harder and faster. He made no attempt to comment on my speculation, but I could see that his face was growing paler with every word I uttered.

"Maybe what would happen would be that she simply disappeared for a few days until the injury was healed. That would make sense, wouldn't it?"

The rag fell from his hand and he left it where it had fallen on the floor. Still he didn't look up at me or answer me. Mama had tried to help his wife, continued to try to help her. Jed would not admit to anything she might be doing that was likely to get her in trouble. But I knew then. Without a doubt, I knew. And the thought terrified me, as much as it obviously did him.

Her rides had to be stopped, but my thoughts were too chaotic to see even a glimmer of a solution at that moment. Temporarily I settled on the only possibility with which Jed might assist me.

"I just want you to know that if on any night you're saddling Antelope, I want to find Lofty saddled as well. I would take it amiss if I came out here and found the one gone and the other not ready to leave. Do you take my meaning, Jed?"

He grunted something that sounded like "Yes, ma'am," and I didn't scold him for his lack of proper manners. I left him rubbing furiously at the brass, muttering imprecations on the hapless chickens he could see pecking outside in the straw.

If I had wanted to join the others in the saloon, I would have had to change my boots, and I couldn't bring myself to do it. As I slipped past the open door, I could hear Amanda playing the pianoforte and singing. She was in particularly good voice that evening, and I felt a twinge of jealousy when I heard Sir John join in with her. Cousin Bret has no ear for music; he was seated on the striped sofa looking bored.

Though I would have given much for a good night's sleep, I had a suspicion that Mama intended to ride out that night. Perhaps it was something about the look of her eyes or the listening way she held her head, but I was convinced she would leave the house as soon as everyone settled down. At least this time I could be sure that Lofty would be ready to go when I needed her.

I spent a considerable amount of time trying to figure out how to keep Sir John from following us. Eventually I chose the most logical method. There were, of course, several keys to the baronet's room, one of them inside the room itself, so that a guest could lock the door. From my previous experience I felt sure that Sir John had never bothered to do any such thing. And if he didn't lock the door, he was unlikely to notice whether or not the key was missing.

So while I could still hear the music coming from

downstairs, I hurried to his room. Though my plan required only opening the door the smallest distance and reaching around it to remove the key, I found myself almost paralyzed when I stood in front of his room. Every time I had tried to do something unnoticed concerning this place, I had failed. By some odd chance would I find that he was in the room now, rather than in the saloon where he belonged?

Just to be on the safe side I knocked very softly. Then, with my heart pounding in my throat, I turned the knob as quietly as possible and pushed the door open. His room was dark. Even the candle was not lit yet for his arrival. I reached around the door and felt for the key in the lock. It slid out easily into my hand, heavy and cold. I felt like a thief, somehow, and quickly drew the door closed behind me.

Because I needed to know how much noise the key would make in locking the door, I inserted it again, on the outside. The first time I turned the key it seemed to make a great, hollow thunking sound when it locked. That would never do. I tried it again, more carefully. This time the sound was softer, but still far too loud for the middle of the night when not another soul would be stirring.

I decided to think about this problem in my own room and hurried down the hall. My bed looked particularly tempting but I refused to allow myself to lie down upon it even for a moment. Instead, I dismissed Milly and set about donning my darkest riding costume. Only the boots gave me trouble, as Dutch kept nudging me off balance while I tried to put them on.

The dog was an inspiration, though. He tended to wander around the house at night if he wasn't shut in my room. And occasionally he would give one of his gruff barks, not really enough to awaken someone, just enough to cover the sound of a bolt slipping into place. I could get him to bark if I made him sit up for some food. Of course, there wasn't so much as a radish in my room, so I had to sneak down to the larder to swipe a piece of meat. Mrs. Cooper was just putting off her apron and very nearly caught sight of me as I squeezed past the open kitchen door.

By the time I heard the rest of the company going off to bed, I had finally managed to get everything together. There was still a considerable wait until things settled down and became quiet. I kept to a position in that hallway where I could see when the light went off under the baronet's door. Even then I hesitated, though I was having the devil of a time keeping the basset hound from wandering off. I wanted Sir John to be in bed and fallen asleep, if possible, before I acted.

With the greatest caution I inserted the key in the lock, keeping Dutch close beside me by allowing him to smell the meat. He became excited and wanted to have the treat right away, nuzzling my boots and thrusting his cold nose under my skirt. I was terrified that Sir John would hear all the little scrapings and scratchings and come to his door to investigate. So I quickly positioned the key with my left hand and held the meat up in my right.

On cue, Dutch gave out a deep wolf of a bark, and I turned the key. Dutch was so beside himself by now that I feared he would continue to bark and I stuffed the food in his mouth without further ado. The sound of the key turning had been minimal, but I raced down the corridor with Dutch close behind me, just in case the baronet came to investigate.

Nothing happened. I felt sure that if Sir John had heard anything he would immediately have bounded out of bed and tried to get out of his room. When there was no alarm raised, no fists pounding on the solid wood door, I relaxed the slightest bit and allowed myself a small word of congratulation. It was no mean trick, outsmarting our wily visitor.

·12·

Of course, it would all have been for nothing if Mama did not choose to ride out that night. I went down to the back hall as I had the previous night, but this time I sat in the shadow of the door rather than lying down under the table, where I might have fallen asleep. In a surprisingly short time Mama appeared in her black cape and mask, still tugging at a shirtsleeve that had gotten caught under her coat. She passed by my hiding place without a moment's hesitation, so I felt confident that she hadn't seen me. I suppose I could have stopped her then, but I really had to see what she would do.

She moved with surprising speed. By the time I'd given her a little lead, I couldn't see her at all. But when I arrived at the stable I could hear her horse shuffling outside. I slipped in the back way and, thank heaven, Jed had Lofty saddled and waiting for me, though he was nowhere in sight.

As soon as I heard Antelope move off toward the home woods, I led Lofty outside and mounted from the block. No one else was in evidence. There was an almost full moon, fortunately, and a silvery light-frosted night scene. It even glinted off the metal of Antelope's bridle as Mama rode her straight into the woods.

I was keeping a close eye on her, even as I secured my booted foot in the stirrup. By my calculations, she

155

entered on the second path from the right, which led fairly straightforwardly through the woods and came out near the Cambridge Road. It was my understanding that the masked highwayman usually struck on the Newmarket Road, and I was a little surprised by this direction, but I set Lofty off at a good pace in pursuit.

For the better part of an hour I followed Mama, always able to keep her in sight. In fact, it was so easy to keep her in sight that I began to suspect that she knew she was being followed. Perhaps she had known on the occasion when Sir John had followed her, and had led him on a merry chase.

Because she was doing much the same with me. We didn't head straight anywhere. She meandered through the woods, and then through the meadow, and then along the road. I would have sworn, had it not gone midnight, that she was merely out for a pleasant jog. Antelope was good in the dark places like the woods. She never seemed to stumble or put a foot wrong. Lofty was not as sure of herself, but she had a big heart, the darling. My respect for her grew as we wandered along behind Mama.

I cannot say why it never occurred to me that I might not be the only one to follow Mama that night. Oh, I had locked Sir John in his room, but that didn't mean that no one else from the household could get out. Yet it wasn't until we were well along the Cambridge Road that I realized someone was behind me!

The next thing I noticed was that I was being followed by not one but two people. When I cautiously turned my head at a bend in the road, I could distinctly see two horses, each with a rider. One of these people was slight, which led me to identify him as Cousin Bret. Also, against my express wishes, he was riding Thunder, and not always on the road because of our meandering path.

In the moonlight it was impossible to identify the

last rider in our procession, but I was fairly certain of the horse. Apollo had a distinguishing blaze on his forehead that I could see even from this distance. Really, it was too much. How had Sir John gotten out of his locked room? And so fast. I might as well not have bothered going to all that trouble.

There was something strange about the whole business. Mama seemed to know that she was being followed. And I knew we were being followed. So what was the purpose of it all? Did the men really think she was going to rob someone with all of us trailing after her? Or weren't they aware that she had figured out about being followed?

In either case, I decided not to let such a chance pass by. At the next opportunity to disappear from view for a few moments I made my dark cloak look more like a cape in the way it was draped. Also, I managed to smash my hat down with a good whack to make it flatter, the way Mama's was. Amanda would have had an attack of apoplexy if she had seen me do it! There was nothing I could do to make it look like I wore a mask, except draw my hair forward across my face so the pale oval wasn't obvious in the moonlight.

Then, when I was sure that both of them could see me and that Mama was out of sight, I rode Lofty into the forest. Since the two of them were so much farther behind me, I hoped they would think both of us had headed in, if indeed they knew they were following two people. At the distance they kept it was just barely possible they hadn't seen Mama ahead of me.

As soon as I rode into the forest, I knew it was a mistake. Honestly, it was totally black in there, and Lofty immediately became skittish. It was not the same as following where another horse led. She sidled and stomped and shook her neck, just as though she were seeing something that I wasn't able to see. It reminded me forcefully of Mama's ghosts.

To help calm us both, I talked to her as we wove our way through the trunks. "Good girl," I said firmly, patting her neck. "There's nothing the matter, you see. Nothing around us at all." But I could not rid myself of the feeling that there was indeed something there. I told myself that it was only small animals disturbed by our unusual venture into the forest at this hour, but the eerie feeling wouldn't leave me.

I rode deeper into the woods for some time before I heard one of my two followers behind me. Try as I would, I couldn't make out that there was more than one. But it was dark and there were all those trees between him and me. I couldn't possibly tell. Nor could I tell where I was going.

Eventually I turned right, which would take me back in the direction I'd come, but parallel to the road. I had begun to wonder where Mama was and why it had seemed such a good idea to take off into the forest. I was able to keep going only because I felt certain that I wasn't alone. Cousin Bret or Sir John, and possibly both of them, were following me. Besides, what other choice did I have?

I rode for perhaps another quarter of an hour, with Lofty stepping along as though she were the bravest of animals, except that she shied each time an owl hooted or a small, furry animal scurried past her. I did not feel at all courageous myself, but there wasn't much I could do. When I looked back, I saw that there was still one horse following me, but in the dimness I couldn't tell who it was.

And then, after a while and without my realizing when it had happened, there wasn't even the one horse and rider behind me. Once I turned and looked back and saw the movement, decided movement of a horse, and the next time there was nothing except trees and more trees.

It was awful to think that I was alone in those woods. I wasn't frightened for Mama, because she knew where she was going and because at least one of the gentlemen had followed me. But I was alone and it was dark and spooky. Not that I'm generally afraid of the dark. But this was not at home, and I hadn't, in truth, the least idea of where I was. There seemed to be a patch of mist here and there, like a ghost floating in the forest.

And there were sounds that seemed to me unlikely to be little animals and birds. Mysterious sounds, like the ones I suspected the red Indians in the colonies made, calling to one another, identifying a vulnerable stranger in their midst. Not that I feared there were Indians in the forest. I knew better than that! The feeling grew on me that there was someone out there, though, and I could feel my skin shudder under my warm cloak. I continued to ride along, of course, probably communicating my fears to my horse, who became more and more disturbed.

Poor Lofty! She is the sweetest mare and it was worrisome to have her twitching like a toad and sidling right away from the direction I urged her in. I could see her eyes rolling wildly when she tossed her head, too, and it merely made me more frightened. One of the suspicious noises rose louder than ever among the trees, seeming to echo endlessly back and forth from right to left, forward and back, around and around.

Now my hands were trembling, too. Surely this had to be some human . . . with no Sir John or Cousin Bret behind me to protect me from whatever evil lay there.

Obviously the thing to do was to head back to the road. When I tried to turn Lofty's head in that direction, she came closer to balking than I have ever experienced. But in the end I was able to urge her on, forcing her against her will to make this excursion into the depths of blackness. Really, it was no blacker that way than the direction in which we were headed, but she seemed ever so much more hesitant about going there. My skin had begun to crawl and I wished that I were home in my own bed, with the covers up over my head and a candle burning on my nightstand.

Poom! Something leapt out of the dark at us. I screamed in my fright, louder and louder. I could not seem to catch my breath. Something human had lunged from the trees and wrapped itself around me, dragging me from my horse. Lofty took off like the hounds of hell were after her. My fate was sealed. There was no way I could escape when my horse had disappeared through the gloom and I was left in the clutches of a madman.

Well, as is apparent from my writing this, I did survive. I was too shocked for the longest time to hear Sir John saying, "Calm down, Catherine. It's only me. I didn't mean to give you that great a scare. Though God knows you deserved it, my girl. What the devil do you think you're doing out here?"

I have never, without exception, been more relieved in my life. Nor more angry. That is the common result when an incident of this nature occurs. At first you are relieved to find that you aren't in danger, then you are mad as a hornet that someone caused your fear . . . and made you look like a fool. So it's a very lucky thing that he had me in such a tight grip, else I would likely have scratched his face or pummeled his chest in my distress. Not that he needed to hold me quite that closely. After a moment my hysteria lessened and I felt distinctly other than either relieved or angry.

The man is a devil, no doubt about it. He rocked me with his laughter and made fun of my screaming and my fear. And then he kissed me, and kissed me, and kissed me until I was breathless. His lips were cool and sweet, and so demanding that I thought he would gobble me right up. Perhaps he hadn't been so unaffected by my performance, after all. For he clung to me most romantically, whispering my name softly to calm and excite me at the same time.

He was very successful at this. I freely admit it. When he held me pressed against his body, I could feel my own heart race with excitement, and not because he'd frightened me. At the moment I didn't even have the sense to question him about this, I was so taken with his kisses and the warm way his hands played about on my back. There was indeed a warmth spreading straight through me, fluttering in my breast and churning lower down. And that incredible ache that grew with each new onslaught on my lips and my heart. Yes, indeed, he was having a marvelous time arousing me to a frenzy of passion.

Or so I thought at the time, since I had never been moved to quite that state before. What I longed for, I could not quite comprehend, though I knew it was some kind of pleasurable release from this ecstatic pressure. Though I didn't know exactly what was happening, Sir John was considerably more experienced. And just principled enough to spare my maidenly blushes.

What he did, much to my astonishment, was to rub against me in a most enjoyable way. My excitement rose higher and higher until I thought I would burst. And then, to my astonishment, I did burst! Gasping with the enormity and the pleasure of it, I clung to him as though my life depended on him. And he laughed.

Oh, not a mean laugh. I was not at all offended. He laughed with the delight of my responding that way, I think. And he kissed me quite tenderly and hugged me forcefully against him. ''My precious highwayman, you are even more charming than I had suspected,'' he murmured.

''I am not a highwayman,'' I said as sternly as I was able.

''Then what are you doing here in the middle of the night dressed as you are?''

Somehow I still could not tell him about Mama. Whether I did not entirely trust him or thought he would not believe me, I cannot be sure. ''Well, I was restless this evening. I couldn't sleep, you see. And it seemed just the thing to have a bit of a ride on Lofty. Drat, where has she gone? You've scared her off, you villain.''

''Too awful of me, to be sure. You shall just have to ride with me on Apollo. I can't think of much I would prefer more.''

There was a decided gleam in his eye that tempted me to go without a murmur, but my maidenly modesty reasserted itself and I made at least an attempt to find Lofty. I called out for her, hoping that she was still within the sound of my voice. She's ordinarily very good about not straying too far, but she'd been badly frightened. There was no response to my calls.

''She'll be back at the stables by the time we get there,'' Sir John assured me as he tossed me up onto Apollo's back. He had had the forethought to tie Apollo to a tree. When he loosened the reins and held them lightly in his hands, I was tempted to ride off on Apollo, leaving him there. Fortunately my memory of the darkness of the forest made me refrain.

Sir John swung up behind me and shifted us about until I was pretty well sitting on one of his legs. This must have been rather uncomfortable for him, but he never said so. He just told me to lean back against his shoulder and he would get us home in no time.

''What about . . .'' I couldn't mention Mama, I remembered, so I finished, ''Cousin Bret?''

"He decided that the woods were no place to ride in the middle of the night and took off back for the road ages ago. I imagine he's safely back in bed by now."

"And why do you think he was following me?"

"Because he wants to prove that you're a highwayman, Catherine. With that kind of ammunition he can blackmail your family into just about anything. Can't you see how truly desperate a situation you could put your family in?"

I huffed and I puffed and eventually I grudgingly admitted that I could indeed comprehend the danger of the situation. I agreed not to go about robbing people anymore. I even agreed to return the spoils, when he pressed me.

"Tonight?" he asked.

"What do you mean, tonight? Of course I can't return the spoils tonight."

"You could return mine."

Good heavens, I'd momentarily forgotten that he was one of Mama's victims. "Just what was it I took from you?" I asked, assuming he would realize that a highwayman could not be expected to keep straight all of her ill-gotten gain.

"Well, let's see. You took my purse with fifty pounds, and my watch that was my grandfather's, and you took my companion's fan because it caught your eye."

"Surely you jest!" I exclaimed before I could stop myself. No fan has ever held the least fascination for me. But I could imagine Mama being entranced with such an item, since the value of his purse wouldn't have impressed her at all. Not that Mama is necessarily interested in such things, either, but it must have made a nice change from the male items she usually claimed. Very few ladies are on the roads at night.

In any case, I tried my best to recover. "I only take

fans from women who don't seem to deserve them,''
I said severely. ''You must have been with a particularly unacceptable female for me to be interested in
her fan.''

''Don't you remember the occasion?''

I waved aside the question as frivolous. ''It's dark,
you know. And I'm not ordinarily faced with women
and their fans. You thought I must have felt a special
attraction to you, I daresay.''

He chuckled and drew me a little closer with one
arm. ''I'm surprised you didn't.''

In order to make this distraction truly work—in other
words, to keep him from reverting to the subject
again—I gave him a little kiss. Since he was ordinarily
the one doing the kissing, and I the returning of the
kisses, this rather surprised him, but he seemed
pleased. ''You have a very satisfactory way of showing
this attraction of yours,'' he said.

The horse stirred restlessly, but stopped when Sir
John drew on the reins and we clung together for a
while, our lips scarcely parting. After a very long,
breathless time, Sir John drew back and growled, ''At
this rate we will never get back to Hastings, my dear.
And I think you are very much in need of your bed.''

I didn't try to dissuade him from continuing on our
way. It was, after all, deep in the night, and the stable
boys might become alarmed if Lofty arrived there
without me. I became almost eager to get back, not
wanting them to mount a search party for me. And of
course I wondered where Mama had gotten to and
whether or not she would have returned before me. I
devoutly hoped that she wasn't at that very moment
off ordering someone to stand and deliver.

We rode in silence through the silver of the forest,
reclaiming the ribbon of road after a while, where Sir
John set Apollo to a gallop. It was exhilarating, riding
on that powerful beast with Sir John's arm about me

and the warmth of his body pressed against mine. I think I could have remained that way forever. When we rode into the stableyard there was absolutely no one around. I had come to expect, or fear, that half the household would have been roused and ready to ride off in search of me, but there was no one at all.

Lofty wasn't outside by the door, either. We discovered that she had been unsaddled and rubbed down and returned to her box. Really, I was rather indignant with Jed for so casually dismissing my absence. I didn't dare say so to Sir John, however.

"Where's your groom?" he demanded, his eyes flashing with anger. "Surely he didn't go off to bed when you were missing."

My mind worked a little faster then than it had earlier in the evening. I retorted with some confidence, "My groom is instructed to await my horse, not me. I dismount from Lofty while still in the shadow of the trees, my dear fellow. You wouldn't expect me to clatter into the stable yard at this hour, would you? That would attract a definite attention that I don't wish."

Sir John didn't look as though he believed me, but he didn't protest further. I greatly feared that he intended to speak with Jed in the morning, but then I remembered that Jed was very closemouthed about these proceedings. I breathed a sigh of relief about that, and about the fact that both Thunder and Antelope were back in their boxes.

Sir John frowned at me and finished caring for Apollo before taking me by the arm and leading me to the house. He marched me directly up to my bedroom and waited for me to enter, just as though he were afraid that I'd disappear on him again.

"Go in and get into your nightclothes," he instructed. "Then climb into bed and call to me. I'm not leaving here until I see you safely tucked in bed."

While I'm not in the habit of taking orders from the

likes of Sir John, I wasn't in any condition to refuse him what he wanted. I nodded silently and passed through the door, dropping my riding costume on the floor before I remembered that my maid would surely wonder what it was doing there.

Eventually I was in bed and called to him, convinced that he would have taken off for his room long ago, but I watched as the door opened and he came through, looking very dashing and like a highwayman himself.

Nothing would do for him but to walk straight up to my bed and assure himself that I was indeed wearing my nightdress, and quite a modest one at that, of heavy flannel, which came to my wrists and high on my neck. "Now see that you stay there," he said. "Do I have your promise not to leave this bed again tonight?"

"Certainly. I'm too tired to move a muscle, let alone climb out of bed. Thank you for bringing me home— but not for scaring the daylights out of me."

"You're welcome. Sleep well. Good night, my sweet," he whispered as he leaned over to kiss me. "We'll talk more in the morning."

I knew there was something important that I wanted to ask him, but I was so exhausted that my mind had become a blank. He must have left the room then. I wouldn't know because the moment I closed my eyes, I was fast asleep.

Because I didn't know what to tell him, I avoided Sir John the next day. What if he pressed me hard about my activities? What if he wanted me to produce the spoils of my highway robbery right then? I needed time and patience to get all that information from Mama. And even more time and patience to deal with my own jumbled feelings from the previous night's experience. I didn't dare encounter the baronet. The easiest thing to do for the time being was to spend all of my time with Amanda.

Though this surprised her, she could not very well, being Amanda, send me about my business. She did suggest that there might be some things I needed to see to at the stables, but I assured her that everything was under control.

This actually wasn't an untruth, as I'd slipped out there first thing in the morning to see that all of the horses were all right, that is, all the ones that had been ridden out the night before. Jed refused to answer any of my questions. He was very polite in telling me that he most certainly couldn't quite remember whatever it was I needed to know.

When I was with Amanda, Sir John approached us on no less than three occasions. But Amanda had not gotten over the annoyance she felt with him for being a rake, so she gave him short shrift. I was impervious to his suggestions of strolls about the grounds, or accompanying him on an expedition to look at horses for Robert, or any of the other tempting devices he used to try to lure me away.

"You'll have to excuse me, Sir John," I told him, stiff as a poker, the third time he approached. "My head is aching abominably today and I don't at all feel up to entertaining company."

Amanda considered this a rude way of dismissing him, but since she had gotten the idea—heaven knows where!—that I was as annoyed with him as she was because of his rakish reputation, she was willing to overlook my behavior, rough as it was.

Sir John wheedled. "I know just the thing to cure the headache," he assured me. "A walk in the shade, a quiet moment in the arbor on the swing. Just what you need to feel better in no time."

"Ordinarily I would agree with you, but today I cannot see my way clear to accepting your invitation.

You must allow me to be the best judge of my own health.''

''By no means!'' he exclaimed, trying mighty hard to appear in a jovial frame of mind. ''I have had great experience in treating young ladies for the headache and I am guaranteed to succeed.''

Amanda, of course, was horrified by this declaration. She considered it an outright admission of his dalliance with any number of young ladies, and her skin paled right before our eyes. Her voice, chilly before, now turned positively frigid. ''Catherine will do best to stay with me on this occasion,'' she said. ''Mama would wish it that way.''

Though Sir John desisted after that, he did whisper a threat into my ear as he departed, when Amanda's attention was distracted by Cousin Bret's arrival. ''You'll not manage to avoid me forever, my girl. And you'd better be ready to do a lot of explaining.''

Cousin Bret was as determined to get Amanda alone as I was not to be left alone with Sir John. Amanda didn't want me to leave her, I could tell, but it was important that I learn what he was up to and how much damage he could do. So I tactfully excused myself and went to listen at the open door onto the balcony.

·13·

Perhaps fearing that he would be interrupted, Cousin Bret got straight to the point. "You must have some idea of how attached I have become to you, dear Cousin Amanda. May I call you Amanda?"

"Why, no, that would be most improper," she protested, backing away from him. "And I don't at all know what you mean by saying you've become attached to me. You know you've always been made welcome here as one of the family, but I don't think it would be wise of you to form any particular attachment. We are close family, and that is surely tie enough."

Poor Amanda. I could almost have pitied her, except that Cousin Bret had probably never gotten the full brunt of her tongue when she was offended and I wished to hear her exhibit it to him. Unfortunately, he wasn't waiting for anything more promising to come from her lips. Better to convince her of his hold before she had a chance to say too much.

"You haven't any idea how close a tie I have to your family," Cousin Bret remarked. He was playing with a snuffbox, flipping the lid open and then snapping it shut. Perhaps he regarded this as a sophisticated thing to do; I could see that Amanda merely found it irritating. After a moment she grabbed it from his hand, as one might with a persistently annoying child, and stuffed it in the pocket of her apron.

'I shall return it later,'' she told him. ''Now I think we had best terminate this conversation before more is said that should be left unsaid. Let me assure you that I am perfectly satisfied with arrangements the way they are.''

''But I am not.'' The disappearance of his snuffbox had roused his ire and I thought for a moment he intended to grab it back from her. It would have been an awkward business, but that is not above Cousin Bret.

Still, he was even more determined to have his way over the conversation, so he motioned her to a chair and she, out of some sense of politeness, I suppose, took it. He seated himself with a most insufferable assurance, crossing one skinny leg over the other and waving it in a disastrously amusing fashion.

''As you know, I am to come into my father's property upon his death. However, as your brother will be heir to the earl, I think he would not be averse to giving Hastings to me. On the best authority, I have it that it is not presently entailed.''

Amanda stared at him. ''Give you Hastings? Your wits have surely gone begging, Cousin Bret.''

''Not at all. I think when your brother hears of the goings-on here he will be more than pleased to relinquish his estate to keep them quiet. I could easily have the earl's ear, too, you know.''

Amanda hadn't the slightest idea what he was talking about. She frowned with perplexity and then seemed to hit on the obvious explanation. ''You cannot mean Sir John and Catherine! I'm sure there is nothing improper about their discoursing with each other on occasion. Sir John's reputation is bad, to be sure, but he wouldn't dream of inflicting himself on my sister. Why, she's a young woman of quality.''

Now it was Cousin Bret's turn to wonder where the conversation was going. "I'm sure I don't care a fig for what Cousin Catherine and Sir John do. They're both too ramshackle for words, if you want my opinion."

After all the time I'd spent trying to be affable to Cousin Bret, this was how he repaid my efforts! Unconscionable.

But he was continuing. "Don't be a peagoose, Amanda. We're talking about your mother's 'adventures.'"

Amanda obviously hadn't the slightest suspicion of Mama's affairs. She stared at our cousin with the frown that had become a permanent feature on her face during this interview. I could tell when she hit on the idea that he was talking about Mama's conversations with ghosts. Well, poor girl, what other evidence did she have of her own mother's problems?

"Mama has a slight nervous disorder," she acknowledged graciously. "It is the result of Papa's dying so suddenly and leaving her all alone. You mustn't think that it is something that will last forever. It has only been a year since Papa's death and she will recover in time."

Cousin Bret obviously thought she was talking about Mama's highwayman act. "You have done nothing, yourself, to put an end to this, I take it?" he asked, almost incredulous.

"Well, what is there that I can do? She's not just of the easiest disposition to be culled into a more ordinary frame of mind."

"But the consequences! I assure you that I would put a period to it if I were in charge of Hastings."

Amanda stared at him. "You would do nothing of the sort. It is Mama's own choice, what she wishes to do. And you are not going to be in charge of Hastings. Pray put that thought from your mind."

"That's not the only thought I have in mind," Cousin Bret assured her. He swung his leg a little faster now. He'd gotten to the real meat of the conversation. "I think," he said in his most sinister voice, "that it would be well for the two of us to marry."

I wanted to run in there and slap his face for such impertinence. Amanda's color rose high in her cheeks, her nose seemed to become longer and sharper, and she stared at him with painfully cold eyes.

"I'm sure I cannot think where you came to believe that I would be agreeable to such a proposal, but I beg that you will disabuse yourself of the notion instantly. Nothing could be farther from my mind than a marriage with you. There has been no suggestion in my behavior that I would welcome such an offer. In fact, I have just spent a certain amount of time warning you from making it."

She leaped up from the chair, only to be followed by him as she raced for the door. Fortunately, it was not the door were I stood, but the one into the hall, and it was partially open, so that she could call for help, of course, should anyone attack her. That's the purpose of all doors left open in a young woman's presence, I assume.

Cousin Bret restrained her with a hand on her sleeve. Amanda didn't dare pull away for fear of ripping her best day dress. Poor lamb. I could sympathize with her confusion over the situation. She plucked desperately at his fingers, trying to remove them from the light fabric, but he persisted, twisting the material between his fingers in an excess of excitement.

"I'm afraid you don't understand. I can force you to marry me," he told her.

Her astonishment was considerable. Her eyes widened with incredulity and her fingers fluttered into little butterflies that moved round and round her neck. "You must have lost your mind. If you let me go this instant, I will not tell Mama. Otherwise, I shall be forced to speak with her, and she will find it necessary to insist that you leave the house. Really, something has happened about which you should see a medical man, Cousin Bret. Your brains have become overly active, or you have been reading gothic novels. Gentlemen do not force ladies to marry them, and if you have taken the notion that they do, you are much mistaken.''

Cousin Bret had still not let go of her dress, but Amanda was so agitated that she pulled away from him and I heard the fabric rend. ''Oh, now look what you have done!'' she cried. ''It can never be repaired and it is my very favorite. Alice said that I don't look so well in any other gown and now I shall have to find something new to wear. Oh, you wicked, wicked man.'' And she took off at a run, pushing open the door and racing out into the hall and up the stairs.

Cousin Bret just stood there, looking as though something had happened that he did not at all comprehend. He frowned and stomped his foot and took to pacing about the room. For a long time he wore a path on the Axminster carpet, up and back, up and back. His hands were clasped behind his back and his head down; he looked the perfect caricature of a man distressed.

I hadn't the least pity for him. Imagine his trying to blackmail dear Amanda. Probably it was a very good thing that she hadn't the slightest idea of what he was saying. Save for the necessity of keeping my own knowledge a secret, I would have raced into the room and confronted him.

As I was crouched there on the balcony, Sir John came upon me and expressed his annoyance with my behavior. ''You really are the most abominable girl, Catherine.''

I couldn't think of a good retort, so I shrugged. He

shook his head in exasperation and placed my hand through his arm. "We need to talk," he said, then he led me to the shrubbery at the side of the house. It was a neglected shrubbery, not one where people strolled very often, because in hot weather it was muggy and in cold weather it was breezy.

Today it was still and breathless. Sir John stood me at arm's length and studied me, his blue eyes searching for some sort of answer to a question he did not bother to frame in words. Satisfied, I suppose, with what he saw, his arms came around me and drew me to him. And his lips were so terribly sweet that I had a difficult time pulling myself away from them, but pull away I did.

"Really, Sir John," I said, straightening and patting down my disordered hair. "It's quite ungentlemanlike of you to handle a poor young lady in such a fashion. Quite improper, as Amanda would be happy to tell you."

"No doubt. But it is a sure way to get your attention, and I want your attention. There are several matters we have to discuss. Such as your cousin's assumption that your mother is the highwayman."

By the close way he surveyed me I knew that he was trying to analyze what effect this statement had on me, but I managed to drop down to dust off my shoe at just the right moment.

"Cousin Bret has never been able to get things quite straight," I assured him. "But you will have to excuse me. I really must get back to the stables and check that Lofty has settled down. She was badly frightened last night."

"Strange. One would have thought she would be used to the dark by this time, with all your nighttime activity." His brows were raised in the most abominably quizzing way.

I hastened to add to my tale. "Sometimes I ride

Mama's horse. Antelope is extraordinarily brave. She's the kind of animal who doesn't seem to notice if it's day or night.''

''I see.'' It didn't really look as if he saw at all.

''Have you anything further to say?'' I asked. ''If not, I shall be about my business.''

He shook his head, not unhappily, but with a measure of frustration. ''Catherine, you simply must learn to confide in me. Have I not laid to rest any suspicions you may have entertained when I first arrived?''

My suspicions had long since been lulled by his kisses and his confessions. But I felt I had to keep him from finding out about Mama. Which would be easy enough, if I could only keep her from riding out at night again, and if I could get her to tell me where she had hidden her ill-gotten gains.

''There's nothing to confide to you,'' I assured him. The question that had bothered me before I fell asleep occurred to me, and I thought it would serve as a good distraction. ''How did you get out of your room last night?''

His mouth broke into a wide grin. ''I liked that,'' he admitted. ''I especially enjoyed the performance with the dog after everything had quieted down.''

''It took excellent timing to manage it.'' I had put on my haughtiest air, but just to heighten his amusement. ''Dutch is not trained to take part in that kind of project and it was hard to keep him at my side. He kept wandering off.''

The baronet laughed and declared that he would have liked to see it. I prolonged the telling about the meat and the turning of the key in the lock for as long as I could, and then I pressed him to tell his side of the story.

''I'm afraid it's nowhere near as exciting as yours. When I came into my room I discovered that the key was missing and I went down to the housekeeper's room and asked for a duplicate.''

I must have looked crestfallen, for he asked, ''Did you think I had climbed out the window and risked my neck slithering down a vine?''

''Well, I thought it would be a little more exciting than getting a key from the housekeeper,'' I sighed. ''After all the work I went to.''

And to make up for my disappointment, he kissed me. I liked his kissing me, but I couldn't help wondering if it was leading anywhere. By our country standards what had passed between us was a great deal more that flirtation, but it seemed less than a courtship—more like the prelude to a proposition that someone of my standing would surely not receive. From Lady Sutton's letter I could imagine Sir John behaving in this fashion with some lady in London whose reputation was not at all what it should have been.

He put me from him gently and said, ''I think it's time we contacted Robert. He'll have more success in determining what is really going on here.''

That would never do! ''You would just upset him. There's no need for him to know because I won't ride out again. I promise you I will never rob anyone again. Besides, Robert couldn't possibly leave London.''

''Oh, I think he could manage to come. Robert is much freer than you all seem to believe. True, his uncle has hog-tied him in some ways, but he has a few escape routes that he has yet to employ. For your own sakes, he had best be informed.''

Now I was thoroughly alarmed. I grasped his hand and pressed it hard, trying to impress him with the enormity of my plea. ''Oh, please don't. I should hate for him to know of anything so . . . so unappetizing about his family. Nothing of this is going to leak out. It's over, and you won't have a worry about it anymore. Wait a few days and see if things don't adjust as perfectly as you could wish.''

He stared at me until I could feel the flush rising into my neck and cheeks. Really, he is the most unaccountable man. Those eyes, blazing down at me, seeming to see right into my mind and perhaps even into my heart. I returned his gaze as steadily as I was able, but it was tremendously difficult.

After a minute or two he released his hand from mine and shook his head. "I'm sorry, Catherine, but I really have to write to him. He has a right to know what's going on at his home, within the bosom of his family.''

His long perusal of me had told him something, though I was not quite sure what. He had made up his mind, and I knew, deep inside me, that he wouldn't change it. I could wheedle or plead and he would feel drawn to me, wishing to please, but he was determined that he had the right of it, and he wouldn't change his mind for me or anyone else.

Though I wanted to cry with frustration, I refused to let him see it. "Very well, I'll just be off to the stables, then.''

"I'll come with you.''

"Thank you, no. I would prefer being by myself for a while.''

"As you wish.''

When I walked away from him, he remained in the shrubbery and I didn't see him again until dinner. Which suited me just fine.

The next afternoon there was a violent thunderstorm and none of us was able to go outdoors. Amanda was practicing the pianoforte and I was wandering around the house, wishing that there was something interesting for me to do. I thought that Sir John had gone off in his carriage and would not be back for some time because he would get caught at the local public house, where he had gone to have a game of darts or some such evidence of manly camaraderie. But suddenly there he was, stomping in the back door, raindrops running down his driving coat and plopping off his curled beaver hat. He looked wonderful, so unaffected and almost naughty.

In the very instant that he looked up to catch my gaze on him, he winked at me. Imagine! A man of his finesse, and he winked at me, just as though I were a parlor maid. Well, I was offended. And I let him know it. My chin went up and my brows rose to their haughtiest level. "I am not accustomed to being treated with such a cavalier want of courtesy," I informed him.

"Aren't you? How very strange. I should have thought everyone would have treated you that way, considering your hurly-burly ways. My dear Miss Ryder, I could think of a more courteous greeting, but then you would not have spoken to me at all. You would have darted off like a deer, as you've been doing for the last day or two. Avoiding me at all costs, and I have discovered the reason!"

"And what is that?"

"Because you have not yet delivered on your promise to come up with the spoils of your robberies."

He said this in a perfectly normal voice, and I looked all around the area, frantic that one of the servants might have heard him. I put my finger to my lips, saying, "Shush, shush. Lower your voice, for pity's sake. Do you want all the world to know?"

"Do you mean they don't? That, too, is a rarity around Hastings, if I may make so bold as to say so. The servants and the family are ordinarily a surprisingly curious bunch."

It seemed safer to change the subject. "You're dripping wet, Sir John. I'll ring for your valet to help you out of those damp clothes and into something dry and warm. Perhaps you would like an extra fire laid in your room. Or you will find one already burning in the library, where we tend to congregate on rainy, chill summer days. It's by far the coziest room on such a day.''

''Oh, I don't think I will need a fire in my room. But I'll change and be waiting for you there in half an hour. That will make a very private place for you to bring the money and purses you've stolen, where no one will see them or you.''

''But I can't very well come there,'' I protested.

''Why not? You've been there on several occasions. Stretch your principles, Miss Ryder. After all, if it is perfectly all right with your principles for you to steal so unmercifully, you should be able to convince your conscience that bringing the spoils to my room is a mere trifle.''

He had a point, of course, and so I agreed. But I didn't really intend to keep to my end of the bargain. One doesn't have to bow to coercion, does one? I would search Mama's room, of course. As I had been unable to get her to speak on the matter of highway robbery, or the goods she had taken, I felt myself justified in searching her room, but I felt the chances of finding the booty were small. Since it was her room, she knew best where something could be spirited away without a servant or a family member happening on it by mistake.

As I watched Sir John take the stairs two at a time, it occurred to me that Mama would not necessarily have hidden the booty in her own room. In fact, seeing that energetic male body bounding upward, I became positively convinced that she had hidden it in my brother's room, since he had not been home in such a long time and was not likely to arrive anytime soon. Unless Sir John was able to convince him to come for

Public Day. When the baronet was out of sight, I followed more slowly and discreetly up the stairs.

Robert's suite was in the same wing as Mama's, which would have made it very handy. And what was even more significant was that Robert, as a child, had devised any number of hiding places for his own treasures. I had managed, over time, to discover all of them. Or so I hoped. Mama would have known where they were, too, because Robert trusted her when he was very small and would have shown them to her, and forgotten later that any growing boy would have done anything so indiscreet.

There was the false back to one of his dresser drawers. A carpenter had built it for him when he was very young. But the false compartment was empty, and I felt a great disappointment. Surely it would have been the simplest place for Mama to hide her stolen treasures. I had a moment's hesitation before I started methodically searching through the other locations.

There was a space under one of the floorboards, which was in turn under the bed. I had to move the bed some distance to uncover it, and I became convinced in the process that this would indeed be the location of Mama's ill-gotten gains. But no. After all the struggle and the attempt to make no noise, all I found in the space was dust and cobwebs. Ah, well, that was only the second possibility.

I proceeded to the deep caverns of the closet, well behind the hunting clothes that Robert had left here when he took most of his wardrobe up to London with him. Nothing. I searched in the dressing room, where there were storage boxes and even a locked cabinet, with no success. Surely Mama would have hidden it here. It was so much safer than her own room. But I could find nothing.

I stood in the middle of the floor, looking about me, wondering if I had forgotten anything. Robert's room is spacious and light in sunny weather when the heavy draperies are pulled back from the windows. Because of the darkness of the rainy day, I had found it necessary to push back the draperies on the western set of windows. There was little point in opening the other set, as they faced north, with several large, leafy trees blocking any light from entering. When Robert was away we kept the draperies closed, to prevent the furniture and carpet from fading in the sun.

The draperies were a royal-blue velvet, quite handsome. Robert had been quietly thrilled when Mama had the room done over many years ago, when he was still a boy. They made him feel grown-up, I think, and almost invulnerable. As I was about to close the western draperies, my mind locked suddenly on the other set of windows.

Because of their placement, those window coverings were probably not touched from one month to the next. I went over to the draperies and began to shift them, reaching for the tie to secure them against the wall. My hand encountered something cold and hard. At first I thought it was merely a knob on which to hook the pull, but I was quite mistaken. When I pushed the folds of velvet out of the way, I found a small box resting at the corner of the windowsill, almost as if it belonged there. It might have contained a boy's treasures and been left there as a reminiscence. Even when the draperies were caught back against the wall, it was hidden from view by the folds.

The lid wasn't even locked. I think perhaps the box itself had been one of the prizes Mama had gained on her adventures, for I did not recognize it. When I lifted the lid, my breath caught in my throat. There were jewels and coins and watches, all of them glittering wondrously in the wet afternoon light. But something else caught my eye. Hanging from the rod above, where it could only be seen from the back, which was

against the wall at this point, were several very elegant
and undoubtedly expensive necklaces. My eyes very
nearly popped out of my head. How very risky for
Mama to leave these things so much in the open. And
yet, until now, they hadn't been discovered. Really, it
was too much.

"So that's where you keep them," Sir John said,
causing me to jump a good foot in the air. Really, the
man had an absolute penchant for frightening people.
And who would have believed that a man so large could
be so quiet on his feet? I hadn't heard a sound. And
yet it was obvious that he's been standing there for
some time. No doubt the surprise of the find had entirely engrossed my attention.

"What are you doing in here?" I asked, defensive
to the death.

"Just trying to recover my losses. What are you up
to? Looking for a necklace to wear this evening, perhaps?"

"That's none of your business," I told him. "Oh, I
wish you would leave me alone. Take whatever is yours
and be off, will you?"

Sir John reached around me and lifted the box from
the windowsill. His breath came in a sharp whistle.
"Good Lord, how long have you been at this game?
Do you go out every night?"

"You know I don't. And I wish you would leave
before I call one of the servants."

"I think you would be ill-advised to call anyone.
Except perhaps your mother."

Had he started to suspect my mother again? Couldn't
the man make up his mind? I wanted him to suspect
no one but me. "Please don't tell Mama. I'll manage
to get everything back to whoever it belongs to, but
you mustn't let her know. It would devastate her."

"Somehow I doubt that." His voice was so dry with
irony that he nearly coughed. "Catherine, isn't it time

you told me the truth about what's going on? When are you going to trust me?''

That was a question that I had come to want answered, too. In some ways I did trust him. As with my heart, I suppose. But did I dare trust him with the family honor, when Mama had actually robbed him? Robert was one of his friends, of course. That would count for something, but I could not tell how much.

''Mama is still disturbed by my father's death,'' I said. I was edging away from the window and the curtains. He might not have seen the hanging necklaces and I didn't wish to draw his attention to them.

When I said nothing more, he looked inside the cache and fingered through the goods, presumably trying to find his own items. After a moment he drew a purse from the pile. As he lifted it, I could distinctly hear the jingling of many coins. He must have been carrying a great deal of money with him at the time. To entertain the young woman, I supposed, and in high style. Me he merely kissed on picnics and when I was out riding in the middle of the night.

''So that's yours, is it? Well, then shut the box and put it back. I'm not going to have you fingering through all the rest of the booty.''

''Do you really call your haul booty?'' He looked intrigued by this possibility. ''Do you call yourself a highwayman, too?''

''Certainly not. I'm an adventurer. Nothing so crass as a highwayman. Only dishonest people are highwaymen.''

''I hadn't thought of it that way. Do you consider it an honest activity, stealing watches and purses from your neighbors?''

''I very seldom steal from my neighbors,'' I insisted. ''At least not the ones I like. Most of them have been strangers, or obviously wealthy enough to sustain a piddling loss.''

"Still, it's not for you to decide where their wealth is to go." He said this sadly, as though the lesson were one he knew I could not understand or would not be able to grasp. Why, the poor man had begun to believe that I was totally immoral. And then I saw the lurking amusement in his eyes and realized that he thought to catch me out in my "confession." I refused to be fooled by him.

"Perhaps not. But I have decided to do it." I swung away from him and motioned him to follow me. "I'm going to lock this door after you've left so that you can't come back in here and remove the purses. You don't, after all, have the first idea to whom they belong. You will have to trust me to return everything on my own."

He eyed me closely for a moment but must have decided that I wasn't going to change my mind. So he left by the dressing-room door and I locked it after him, with a key from the inside of the door. The servants would be confused by finding the door locked, but it wouldn't last for long. I was determined to remove the evidence as quickly as possible from Robert's room and conceal it in my own. No one was likely to look for it there, except Sir John himself, and I planned to protect myself against him.

·14·

As I let myself out of the room and was locking the door, Amanda appeared in the hall and wanted to know what I was doing. It's easy to fool Amanda when you tell her something she wants to hear, so I said, "Oh, I believe Cousin Bret is making a habit of coming into Robert's room and pretending that he's master of the house. I cannot bear to think of it. So I'll keep the doors locked for the time being. Will you tell Lucy? She won't be needing to clean in there for a few days, I should think."

"Cousin Bret is undoubtedly the most unconscionable, despicable, ungrateful, obnoxious person I have ever met in my entire life." Once Amanda got going, she could keep going for some time, and I wanted to distract her, so I allowed her to go on and on about our undesirable cousin.

"Imagine the nerve of him! Thinking that I would consider marrying him. Why, that is the most ludicrous thing I've heard in years. Really, Mama should send him away. I think she is far too generous, allowing him to stay on here for as long as he wishes. Don't you think it would be a good idea if I wrote to Robert and asked him to hint Cousin Bret away from here?"

"Nothing less than a pistol would convince Cousin Bret to depart," I said, thinking that I might be reduced to that, all things being equal. "But you might as well make the effort. Robert will be annoyed, of course, that Cousin Bret has been bothering you, but he will undoubtedly wish to do something about it, and maybe that something will include his coming down here to deal with the matter himself.''

''What a wonderful thought! I shall write to him this instant.''

A woman of her word, she scurried off to find her quill and foolscap, for she liked to write a good, long letter when she had determined to write one at all, which was not very often. Robert complained that he was unable to read half of what she wrote, because she crossed her lines, but it never made Amanda change her style. I wasn't sure it was a perfectly good idea having Robert come down at just this moment, but I figured Sir John would be pleading the case as well, and Mama, and one more effort wouldn't make much difference.

Exhausted by my exertions and by all the stories I'd been forced to invent, I too wandered off to my room, thinking of where I could manage to hide the money and trinkets. At length I determined on the closet, behind several older gowns and hats that wouldn't likely be touched by my maid in the near future. I doubted that Sir John would be willing to search though every article of clothing in my closet, for there were many of them. Things should be perfectly safe there for a while.

Amanda didn't appear until much later in the afternoon, but Cousin Bret had managed to find her as soon as she descended from her room. He was indulging in a type of behavior that he must have considered courtly, but Amanda merely stared coldly at his attempts to be amusing. When Sir John followed me into the room, it was evident that he'd made a decision about Cousin Bret's rights with regard to Amanda.

''I believe your cousin has clearly stated her position with regard to your attentions, Mr. Cummings.

So let us have no more of them.'' With that he turned toward Amanda himself and proceeded to charm her anew with his own brand of amusing tales. I could tell that she hadn't forgotten his bad reputation, but when he was of a mood to be entertaining, it was hard to resist him. Mama arrived in time to hear one of the more scandalous *on dits* that he told, and she tucked her hand under his arm.

''You're a rascal, sir. How very unkind of you to describe the lady as of limited intelligence. Why, I met her years ago and I can tell you that she's nothing of the sort. She hasn't, in fact, a drop of sense or learning.''

With which she gave a merry laugh and warned him that he was only to tell her three more of these tales before dinner would be ready. She looked so youthful and happy when he was talking that for a moment I almost forgot about her midnight activities. But I would have to speak to her. If for no other reason than to be sure that the purloined items were returned to their rightful owners.

And I would have to figure a way to keep her from riding out anymore.

I excused myself just a little early from the evening's amusements. I didn't want it to be so late that everyone would decide to go to bed at the same time, or so early as to make them wonder at my disappearance. I had to claim the headache again, and Sir John regarded me with narrowed eyes, but he made no attempt to obstruct me.

The first thing I did was to search Mama's room. It wasn't terribly difficult to find the cape and mask, which worried me, because it meant that her maid must surely have seen them. My plan was to remove the clothing and hope that she wouldn't ride out without it. For the time being, I placed it in a box under my bed with a tie around it, and a clever insertion in the knot that would tell me if anyone untied it. And if my maid found it, I would simply claim that I planned to wear it as my Public Day costume. Perhaps Mama had used a similar excuse.

There was a light tap on my door just as I was thinking about going to bed. It had not the sound of my maid's hand, nor Amanda's, and I opened the door cautiously. Sir John slipped inside the room just as though I'd invited him. "I wanted to see if you were feeling better," he explained.

Which was not his intent at all. He moved close to me and I was very aware of his nearness. Though I have a certain amount of height, he was several inches taller than I, and seemed to tower over me in the flickering light. His hands came to the sides of my waist and he smiled at me with such force that I almost gasped. What I should have done was to pull away from him then, certainly, and possibly slap his hands as well, but I remained still as a statue, waiting to see what would happen next.

His head lowered to mine and I felt the brush of his lips, so light they might have been the wings of a butterfly, grazing my trembling lips. How very unnerving to have him so close, in my own bedroom. Not that I was afraid of his kissing me. I knew beyond the least doubt that he would never harm me.

Though he was a rake and certain things were more familiar to him than to me, that seemed only to add to my excitement. He was accustomed to the heady sensations that I was so new to. He understood what the yearnings inside me could lead to and how easily they could be satisfied, as they had been the other night.

I understood very little, except that I loved the sensations he created in me. Not that I was entirely ignorant about relations between men and women; I knew there was something more between them than I had yet experienced. But without a real knowledge it's hard to either control or acquiesce to the pull of desire. With his lips on mine and his hands at my sides, I felt almost desperate for closer contact. I pressed my breasts against his chest, hoping to ease the ache somewhat.

"This won't do," he whispered against my hair. "Your brother would call me out at dawn."

"Then we shan't tell him. Surely there can't be any harm in it."

He shook his head in mock despair. "You tempt me, my dear. I really did come to assure myself of your well-being. Or at least to do no more than steal a kiss. Rake that I am, though, the vision of you has overwhelmed me."

He was half-teasing, half-serious. In the depths of his eyes I could see that he was shaken, that the kisses were more than a game, that the feelings of intensity were more than sensual ones. Something about me had captured his imagination, had turned his world upside down—much as mine had been by him. Was it just the wild belief that I was a highwayman?

"Just hold me and . . . kiss me. Surely there can be no lasting harm in that."

He laughed. "Lasting, eh? That depends on what you mean, my dear. It certainly won't corrupt your body, but it may indeed intoxicate you and eat away at your moral fiber." He ran a finger along my collar bone. "You have a very flammable moral fiber, I think."

"My moral fiber is nonexistent right now," I assured him, pressing my body up against his. "How is yours?"

"Temptress! I don't have to accept your challenges. Remember, I am a rake and haven't much moral fiber at all."

"So you won't kiss me?"

"I dare not."

"You rakes are all the same."

"Are we?" His lips brushed against mine and then moved farther down, to nibble at my neck, and then my collarbone and then . . . "And here I thought there must be something special about me to have attracted your attention."

"There is something special about you," I whispered. "And about the way you make me feel. I'm not afraid, and I'm not missish. Please kiss me."

He drew me down with him into the chair, holding me easily on his lap. With his lips he brushed my gown down, down, over the fall of my breast. Kissing me there, where I wanted him to. Kissing me, tasting the soft, smooth skin. Roving with his tongue over the wide expanse and finally coming to the tip of my breast. The moistness, the pressure, the incredible sensations that flooded me very nearly made my knees go weak. The only thing that saved me was that I didn't want it to stop. I wanted his mouth on my breast, on the sensitive nipple, licking, sucking, kissing me, until I could scarcely bear it.

"Oh, Catherine," he breathed.

"Please don't stop," I begged. "Kiss me."

He rolled the nipple between his lips, with his tongue touching it inside his warm, eager mouth. Then he drew on it, tugging, tugging at the very core of me. My heart pounded faster, my hands gripped tightly against his back. The excitement rose in me, and rose, and rose, until I could scarcely believe that my body could bear it. Each time he drew on it, my body responded with a shuddering, desperate longing.

With the palm of his hand he pressed against the spot where my longing had grown most intense. The pressure both relieved and increased the overwhelming desire. His kisses on my breasts became more demanding, the pressure from his palm more intense, until I found myself swamped with waves and waves of ecstasy.

"What's this?" he asked softly, kissing away the tears that coursed down my cheeks. "Tears and laughter both. How splendid! You are the most astonishing woman, Catherine." He cradled me until my body had calmed. Then he kissed the tip of my nose and said, "I don't know how I can bear to leave you. But I must. At any moment your maid is going to knock on the door and I daren't let her find me here."

I stumbled up out of his lap and tried to organize my disheveled clothing. My voice was still rough with emotion when I spoke. "Yes, you must leave. I should have sent you earlier. No, no. I won't even say that. I'm glad you didn't. I'm glad you stayed. Thank you."

He lifted my chin with his finger. "There's no need to thank me, my sweet. It is I who am grateful. Sleep well."

His kiss brushed my lips lightly. In the dimness he moved toward the door, opened it cautiously, and checked the hall for anyone's presence. Then he turned and said very distinctly, "Tomorrow we will discuss this matter of your mother. It can't be delayed any longer."

And he was gone.

So he knew that it was Mama who was the highwayman, after all. I sat for some time trying to determine whether this made any difference to the way he might feel about me. If his affection wasn't caused by his believing that I was a wild, unprincipled young woman, could it possibly just be that he cared for me because of who I really was?

I would like to have speculated on that lovely theory for the rest of the night, but I knew I would have to talk to my mother before I saw Sir John again, so I hurried off to her room, putting thoughts of the baronet firmly from me. I made my way once again to

Mama's room. Even before I knocked I could hear her talking.

I opened the door a tiny bit to see to whom she spoke, but there was no one in the room. It gave me chills the way she walked up and down, continually letting her eyes wander to the bureau, where the ghost was undoubtedly standing. From the way she spoke, I had no doubt that her visitor was Papa.

"You can see how it is with him, Harold," she was saying. "Quite taken with her, he is. But I can't be sure that he's just the right person for our Catherine. She's a headstrong girl, and I've a mind to think he's rather a headstrong fellow as well. Not the perfect combination, as you and I were. Why, who would there be to put a limit to her waywardness? He would indulge her whims and fancies."

She stood there listening for a while, nodding her head. And then she walked up and down the room, frowning. "Yes, I can see that, but you were such a good influence on me. You didn't let me have my head, and it was for the best. At least for propriety's sake."

I could hardly bear to hear her talk to him—and on such a subject! Papa had indeed trimmed her sails. One wonders how Mama would have been, married to the likes of Sir John. And then I had to wonder whether it would be good for me, either. I didn't want to think about it, because I was really quite taken with him and didn't want to doubt that it would be for the best. But there it was. We were both rather untamed people, and in the end wouldn't it be better for him to align himself with someone like Amanda, who would see to his keeping the line? My, how he would hate that!

"Mama!" I poked my head inside the room, startling her. Her hand flew to her heart, as though she'd had a scare, and she blinked at me owlishly.

"Oh, it's you, Catherine." She beckoned me into

the room. "Was it you who took away my, ah, costume?"

"Yes, and I'll not give it back. This has to stop, Mama. Sir John and Cousin Bret both followed us the last time."

"Us?"

"I rode out after you and they followed me."

"How very extraordinary! Was this Tuesday?"

"Yes, Mama. Will you promise not to do it again?"

She nodded her head dreamily. "Your father hates it. Tonight he threatened not to come to me if I continue. Oh, I couldn't bear that." She turned to meet my eyes and I was startled by the fierceness of her expression. "I've been so good all these years, Catherine. I've done what he wanted and what he believed was right. Just once I wanted to do something of my own, something that wasn't good and right and proper. And then this special visitor came to me."

A "visitor" is a ghost, in Mama's parlance.

"Always before, my visitors were people I knew on this earthly plane," she explained. "But this one was different. He was, in fact, an ancestor of your father's. A distant one, to be sure, but still . . . A Royalist officer during the Civil War. He was dispossessed of his estate and took to the high road to sustain himself, as so many of them were forced to do. He only stopped the hated Roundheads, of course."

"Of course," I murmured, unmoved by the poor fellow's plight.

"No, no, it is true. They dressed in Cavalier costume and rode blood horses." She sighed. "I had the crape mask and the horse pistol, but I would have loved to wear a hat like that. I simply could not find one anywhere in the attics. Do you suppose we could make me one?"

I gave her a severe look and she twisted her hands together. "You needn't worry. It was because he was so like your father, how your father should have been. In some secret way I always hoped that when you were all grown and off about your business, Harold would let down his guard a little and we would do exciting things together. When he died, and I realized that could never happen, something snapped in my mind.''

Instead of saying something, because I could think of nothing to say, I squeezed her hand hard.

Mama met my gaze with steady eyes. ''It will be all right. I know very well that now I've talked to him, Will won't come again.''

''His name is Will, your visitor?''

''Will Martin. Such a solid name, such a handsome fellow. He looked exactly as your father would have done that long ago. Like some of the portraits in the gallery.''

''And did he accompany you when you rode out at night?''

A devilish smile appeared on her tired face. ''Oh, yes. He was there, like . . . like a lover.'' This said boldly, defiantly. ''He went with me and told me which road to take, which carriage to stop, when to ride away if there was danger. I felt safe with him there. And now he won't come again.''

I thought perhaps she said this to mislead me until I saw the tears swimming in her eyes. She spread her hands out toward me, palms up. ''What is there left for me, Catherine? You and Amanda will marry soon. Robert doesn't even come down from town to visit us. And one day he'll bring a bride here to displace me. I don't mean to sound maudlin, but what is there left for me?''

''Oh, Mama.'' I drew her into my arms and hugged her tight. ''There's everything. We all love you and we won't disappear from your life. Robert will come again, and it may be a very long time before he marries. And think of the grandchildren. You'll love there being grandchildren.''

She bit her lip to still its quivering. ''Yes. Yes, I suppose I shall. If everyone doesn't expect me to be a proper old lady. If I can be myself. I loved your father, my dear, but I was never really meant to be a 'good' person. I'm more like you than Amanda.''

Since no insult was intended, I took no offense. Instead, I laughed and kissed her cheek. ''Everything will be all right, Mama. But it is very important that you never rob anyone again.''

She drew in a deep breath of air and let it out in a shuddering wave. ''No, I won't rob anyone again.''

''Maybe you could take up cock-fighting or something equally outrageous.''

Mama smiled at me. Her fingers fluttered up to brush back a curl that had fallen on my forehead. ''You're so like me.''

''Yes, I suppose I am, and I'm glad. Just don't take to the high road in search of adventure, I beg you.''

She nodded, but her attention seemed to have slipped from me and I thought she would speak with Papa again, so I slipped quietly away.

Amanda was in my room and she was hysterical. ''Where have you been?'' she cried, vigorously plying an ivory fan that was usually kept in the top drawer of my bureau. ''I've been looking all over for you.''

''I've been with Mama. What's the matter?''

It was obvious that something was the matter. She'd been crying and her mouth was puckered ready for yet another bout. Her hands grasped the fan like talons and she could not resist hopping about on one foot and then the other. ''It's Cousin Bret!'' she exclaimed. ''You will not believe what he has just said to me.''

Though I knew that I would, I indulged her by looking curious and sympathetic. I felt sure she could use my sympathy.

"That beastly fellow has threatened to tell the world that Mama is a highwayman if I don't marry him."

"And what good would that do him?"

"Why, he believes that she is. In fact," she dropped her voice to continue, "he assures me that he has proof that she is."

"Did you ask him what his proof was?"

"Yes, but he merely laughed and said I would see in due course."

"Hmm. What a reprobate the man is."

"But, Catherine, you don't understand! He believes that Mama would actually ride out in the dark and stop people on the road and rob them."

"I realize that's what he believes." I was trying to figure out whether it would be necessary to tell her the truth. What a difficult thing that would be! Amanda is not long on understanding this sort of problem. "You needn't worry about it, my dear," I said reassuringly. "I'll deal with Cousin Bret. With Sir John's help, if need be. What a joy it will be to see our reprehensible cousin leave Hastings for good."

She was pathetically grateful for this reassurance. "So you don't think Mama is a highwayman?"

I raised my brows at her. "It seems highly unlikely."

"But she does talk to ghosts."

"That's hardly the same thing as robbing people at pistol point," I insisted. "Do you really think your mother is capable of that?"

Much as Amanda wished to say no, I could see that she did indeed regard it as conceivable. Poor girl. Well, there was little I could do to eliminate her doubts until I had talked with Cousin Bret. And another idea was forming in my head. It might just be possible to prove to him that Mama was not the highwayman.

Amanda continued to fan herself and hop about the room, trying to achieve a measure of calm but not being entirely successful. "It's because of Sir John," she declared. "None of this would have happened if Sir John had not arrived to upset the household."

"You can't be serious." I took the fan from her destructive hands and placed it safely back in the drawer. "Sir John is not responsible for the actions of either Cousin Bret or Mama. He's here in the country to find a pair for himself, and one for Robert."

"Robert! Now there is the real culprit. If he were here, he could deal with all these terrible things. Why, oh, why does he stay on in London when he knows that we need him?"

"I don't think he knows how much we need him, and it's the earl's doing, I daresay. He has a very tight rein on Robert, with his threat of creating another scandal in the newspapers if Robert doesn't behave as he wishes."

Amanda sighed. "I must admit that it's frightfully embarrassing to have the earl publish those mean-spirited tales about us. Who cares if one of our horses goes missing for a week? I shouldn't like it at all if he made a laughingstock of us when I am in London for my Season."

"Perhaps he will have died by then," I suggested ruthlessly. "Why don't you run along and go to bed, Amanda? I'll see that everything is taken care of."

"But how?"

"I don't know yet, but I'll figure it out. And don't be upsetting Mama with your tales of highwaymen. She won't need to know about that, I think."

"Well, certainly not! Do you suppose it is actually Cousin Bret who's the highwayman? Didn't he arrive here at just about the time the robberies began?"

"Unfortunately, it was a few weeks later. But I think Cousin Bret has a great deal to answer for. Whatever you do, don't agree to marry him. It would make him insufferable, even if you backed out later.''

''Agree to marry him! I should say not!'' Her eyes narrowed. ''How much do you know about that?''

''I listened in on your conversation this morning. Now don't throw a tantrum, Amanda. I suspected what he was up to and I had to confirm my suspicions. You might have been too proud and proper to tell me when you'd turned down an offer, no matter how offensive it was. I'm glad you made an exception in this case.''

''I should say so! He spoke of forcing me to marry him. But I was willing to lay the matter to rest if he never brought it up again.'' She gave a proud toss of her head. ''Well, I shall go to bed. And I'll lock my door, you may be certain. One never knows what to expect around here any longer.''

·15·

I watched Amanda go with some trepidation. What she had said was true. Things had become rather muddled. It was beginning to look as though I would have to find a way to drag Robert down from London, no matter what his situation was. And I wondered if that would influence Sir John's behavior in any way.

The baronet was behaving very much as though he were interested in me, but he had made no promises and asked for no assurances on my part. His actions on first coming were suspect. He had, after all, appeared interested in Amanda then, hadn't he? Well, after the incident at the pond. Every time I thought about the pond, my cheeks still flushed with agony. And yet, and yet . . .

Considering what had happened since, it also gave me the most wonderful feeling of excitement. At the time I'd been annoyed, but now when I thought of Sir John, I could only picture the two of us swimming there together, naked, our pale skin clear in the water, our bodies coming together . . .

I swallowed and forced my mind to other matters, such as restoring Robert to the bosom of his family. Only a drastic event would bring him down to the country. I set my mind to think of something that I could lie about in a letter but that he would intrinsically believe. Would he believe that I was so tempted by Sir John that I was considering eloping with him?

The idea intrigued me. No family could stand to have such an elopement, though truth be told, it was done often enough and covered up, even among the *ton.* But the Earl of Stonebridge could have such a wonderful time with it, writing the most scathing letter to the *Morning Post,* that surely it would be something Robert would try very hard to prevent, should he somehow know. He did, after all, have some idea of Sir John's reputation, presumably.

The more I considered the possibilities, the more I liked the plan. I drew quill and paper toward me and chewed on the tip of the quill for a few moments before I hit on the proper way to handle the matter.

Dear Robert,

You will be surprised to hear from me, since I so seldom take pen in hand. But I wanted to make sure that you would not be coming down to Public Day. Or are you? It is most important that you let me know.

The preparations are well under way but I know you have a thousand obligations in London, so I expect you won't be able to find the time to join us. And, after all, you've been to many a Public Day in your time, haven't you? This one would be no different, and undoubtedly boring for one who is used to the more exciting entertainments of London.

Your friend Sir John is not spending a great deal of time searching for horses for you. He has chosen his own, of course, with my help, and he will be the envy of the *ton* for them, I daresay. He's quite a handsome fellow, isn't he? And so very charming when he decides to make himself agreeable. He tells me that he has never before contemplated marriage and that perhaps this is because the mamas in London know his reputation.

I haven't their advantage! But my friend Lady Sutton wrote and I am able to discount her tales as malicious gossip of the *ton*. Sir John has explained everything to my satisfaction. Not that Mama would approve of him as a husband, I daresay, or even you, though he is your good friend. I understand that men do not necessarily wish their sisters to marry the men they take for their favorite companions.

Now don't worry about me. I will do very well for myself. Sir John is not at all the villain he is made out to be and I'm sure he will take perfectly good care of [scratched out] anyone he chooses to make his bride.

After a while I will see you in London perhaps. When Mama and Amanda come up for the Little Season, that is. Do you know Sir John's family home in the city? He says that his mother absolutely never comes there, that she stays always in the country. And that the staff are quite accustomed to running the place, so that it would be no job at all to oversee such a place.

We'll manage quite well at Public Day, so don't be worrying about us. With so much hustle and bustle, it would be easy to get lost for a while, wouldn't it? But that is just a whim of mine. Of course no one will get lost. All my love, dear brother. Possibly I shall see you sooner than you expect.

Your loving sister,
Catherine

That should well and truly put the wind up him, I decided as I blotted the letter on paper to keep it from smudging. Because Robert is not suspicious by nature, he wouldn't think to look through the thinly veiled suggestions to a prank. Likely he would feel clever in discovering my message in that jumble of artless chatter. Oh, I was very pleased with myself and felt that the letter would do admirably.

The next morning I saw to its posting first thing. I did not trust it to a footman but took it into the village myself and made sure that it would reach Robert by the next morning. Thank heaven for the mail coaches. As I was returning to the house, I came upon Cousin Bret, who was obviously waiting for me.

"I haven't been able to find your sister all morning," he said in an offensively accusing voice. "I made sure she had gone into the village with you."

"I'm afraid not. I haven't seen her since breakfast myself. What was it you wanted with her?"

He gave me one of his coy looks. I swear there is nothing more disgusting than one of Cousin Bret's coy looks. A grown man has no use for such expressions, and I was on the verge of saying so when he distracted my by saying bluntly, "I intend to marry Amanda, and I hope you will not attempt to thwart me."

"I shouldn't think Amanda had the least intention of marrying you, Cousin Bret. You would do yourself a service to forget such an ambition."

"Oh, I think she will have me in the end. It might prove a very necessary thing for your whole family."

If he thought I would stand for his threats, he was quite mistaken. Right there on the path I would have kicked him in the shins if Sir John had not appeared and given me a sharp, warning look. "Humph," I said, and stalked off, leaving the two of them to confront each other.

After the previous evening I felt in charity with Sir John and fully intended to inform him of Mama's confession and assurances of no further highway robbery. But I would have to wait for that. He looked determined to give Cousin Bret a set-down, which I only wished I could stay to hear.

It wasn't all that hard to find Amanda, if you knew where to look for her, which I did. When she was hiding, or sad, or just grumpy, which she never admitted to, she disappeared off to the old greenhouse, which is no longer used for plants. Robert would like to have it torn down, but it's handy for storage. It's such a pretty building, with vines making a delicate tracery over all the glass panels; I'm sure I would quite miss it if it were destroyed.

Anyhow, Amanda goes there, because she has always kept a chair and a little cache of books in one of the nooks. I doubt that she has much to fear in the way of being interrupted, either. The old farm tools left there are awaiting repair and are only rarely retrieved.

So as not to startle her, I called out her name, as though I were hunting for her and had been all around the estate. She appeared around the corner of the building, just as though she'd been walking. Amanda is of the belief that no one knows her hiding place, and rather than be discovered there, she would come out to meet me, like a mother rabbit leading the fox away from her babies.

"What is it you want, Catherine?" she asked, her voice cross but unrepentant. "One would think I would be allowed to have a little time to myself without the whole of the world attempting to search me out."

"You're just lucky Cousin Bret didn't get this far. He's the other one out searching for you."

Her face tightened. "Well, I shall certainly do my best not to find myself in the same room with that dreadful man."

All night I had worried about his claim to have proof that Mama was the highwayman. For the life of me I could not think what he might possess. The costume was safe in my room and the booty was safe in Robert's. I had checked both caches first thing in the morning. My assumption had to be that he was bluffing.

I dusted a cobweb from the sleeve of my jonquil muslin, an attempt to appear wonderfully nonchalant. "It may be necessary for you to go further than that. What would you say to announcing a false engagement?" Her look of astonishment was almost comical. I hastened to explain. "Not to Cousin Bret! To some fictitious gentleman in the next county. Our cousin couldn't expect you to marry him if you were already engaged."

"How can you think me capable of such deceit?" she demanded. "I shall, of course, do no such thing. My own word of refusal is quite enough to damp Cousin Bret's pretensions."

"You must grant me leave to doubt that. He's the most persistent fellow in the world and he believes he has a tool with which to blackmail us."

She regarded me with anxiety. "Mama is not doing something awful, is she?"

"I think you can feel certain that our mother will not ride out to commit highway robbery." I hastened on. "That is hardly the crux of the matter. We must find a way to rid ourselves of Cousin Bret before he tries to cause trouble."

"But how?"

I had seen the old dovecote on my way to find her and now I was struck with a wonderful inspiration. "I have it! The most terrific plan. But I will need your help, Amanda."

"Oh, dear. You know I'm no good at schemes and playacting." She backed away from me toward the greenhouse and was about to smudge her dress on the dust of the windows.

I caught her hand and pulled her along beside me as I walked rapidly toward the dovecote. "You'll do just fine. Just listen to what I have to say. You may remember a discussion we had with Sir John a very long time ago about the location of the key to the back door, that it was hidden outside.''

''Vaguely.''

''Well, we're going to find the key right now, and all you have to do is make certain you tell Cousin Bret about it.''

Her brow puckered with confusion. ''But how will I be able to do that?''

''It will be simplicity itself. When he asks you to walk with him, you will steer a course toward the dovecote and, as if idly, reach your hand out to check for the key, which you will look at with amusement and tell him the story of how our brother used to let himself into the house with it late at night.''

''What possible good could that do?''

''Trust me. It will be enough, if I am able to manage my end of the matter.''

''And what is that?''

''Nothing that would be of the least interest to you, I assure you.'' Amanda was perfectly satisfied with this statement. She has practically no curiosity at all.

''But what if Cousin Bret doesn't wish to walk with me?''

This was pure fantasy. ''Cousin Bret will walk anywhere with you. Just lead him in the right direction.''

She sighed. ''Very well, if it's that important.''

''It is. Do not fail me.''

The seriousness of my tone must have impressed her. She looked anxiously into my face for a long moment, and then nodded. ''Very well. I'll do as you say. Though I shan't at all like to walk with Cousin Bret.''

When I had left her I went into the house and found the key to the strongbox in the attic. Everyone knows about the strongbox key because we have a family joke about it. The key is astonishingly large for such a use and it has the initials SB on it, just as though they belonged to a person. Mama had laughed about it from the moment she came to Hastings as a bride. The strongbox key would do very well for my plan, since it would be easy enough to make it disappear without anyone realizing what I was about. And the strongbox itself made a terrific hiding place.

Sir John waylaid me as I was going back into the house, and guided me rather firmly down a sunny path leading away. "Where are we going?" I demanded, two or three times. But all he would say was, "You'll see." He didn't seem particularly annoyed with me, so I quickened my pace to keep up with him and hoped we didn't have too far to go.

When we were out of sight of the house, I began to give him sultry, smoldering glances. At least, that is what I hoped they were. His lips twitched with amusement and he muttered something about my being the most provoking girl he'd ever met. Well, I wasn't about to disagree with him because I secretly suspected that he liked being provoked, in more than one way. We trotted on past the open pond and right up to the rocks hiding the secret one. He made a cursory inspection of the area and then waved me along to follow him. We arrived in the glade with our shoes in hand and our feet making wet patterns on the warm rocks.

"I don't know how I resist you," he sighed, drawing me into his arms in a most charming way. "One would think that you had some kind of spell over me. Just what is this web you weave, my dear child?"

"I am not your dear child. I'm nearly twenty-one years old and quite a grown woman."

"I remember." He smiled reminiscently and suggested that we sit on the rocks.

When I had seated myself, he gazed off at the trees

and said in a thoughtful voice, "Your cousin is convinced that your mother is the highwayman, and I must confess that I've had to reach the same conclusion. It could have been you, except that there are too many clues pointing to your mother—Antelope, for one."

"And another?"

His lips twisted ruefully. "Your mother, touched as she is by the spirits of the dead, is simply the more likely person to go out and rob folks on the high road. But you will have to explain to me what you were doing out the other night."

"I meant to follow her. And then, when I found that I was being followed, I determined to convince both you and Cousin Bret that I was indeed the highwayman."

"Why?"

"I think I had some idea of protecting Mama. We've had a long talk now, she and I. It won't happen again. It was one of her ghosts, a Cavalier relative who looked like Papa but offered her a chance for some excitement and adventure." I shrugged. "I don't suppose you would understand."

"Well, not perfectly," he admitted, "but I have a great deal of sympathy for your mother. Our problem now is that Cummings says he has evidence of her robberies. Is it possible that he's found her store of booty?"

"No. The room is locked and none of the purses is missing." It gave me chills even to mention the robbed items that way. More than anything I just wanted them out of the house and returned to their rightful owners. "How are we going to get rid of those things?"

"I've been thinking about that." His arm had come around my shoulders and he drew me close to him. "I doubt if your mother is going to know to whom everything belongs. But the village constable will have had each incident reported to him. We'll hide everything in some safe location in the village and send an anon-

ymous note to the constable. He can find it, return the
goods, and get all the praise. How does that sound?''

I felt so wonderfully safe and protected in his arms.
The most I could do was nod.

"And what shall we do about your cousin?" he
asked.

"I have a plan for Cousin Bret.'' I hadn't intended
to tell him, but I had told him everything else and I
realized suddenly that I trusted him completely. There
was something so strong and honest about him that I
wondered I had ever doubted his sincere desire to help
my family. He had always wanted to help Robert, and
he had come to want to help the rest of us, with his
sympathy for Mama's foibles and his acceptance of
Amanda's correctness, and his . . .

Was it love for me? I couldn't tell. All I knew then,
looking into his deep, intense eyes, was that I loved
him. And I would share my plans with him. I would
have been willing to share a great deal more than that
with him—if only he had asked.

Later we separated before we reached the house, Sir
John to ride Thunder and me to carry out my plan for
the strongbox and the booty. He had allowed as how
my plan might work, and that I had a perfect right to
carry it out, at least these initial stages, on my own.
How delightful it was to find a man who didn't balk at
the slightest irregularity. Really, I considered myself
most fortunate.

I found the strongbox key right where it always was,
and made my way to the attics, where the strongbox
was in its usual place, surrounded by other wooden
boxes and wardrobes containing old clothes. Nothing
could have been better for my purposes.

Leaving the strongbox open, I returned to the hall
outside Robert's room and ascertained that there was
no one about. Too bad I hadn't had the opportunity to

put the items in my closet as I'd planned. It would have felt a lot more comfortable working there.

I let myself in with the key and went quickly to the draperies. The room was dim and had the faint air of a closed space, stuffy and airless. I would have liked to open the windows and let a fresh breeze in. But I couldn't take the time. I felt an urgency about removing the stolen goods.

As I was working the necklaces off the drapery rod, I heard a distinct sound in the corridor outside. My hand froze where it was, lifted high to clutch the cool string of pearls. Suddenly the doorknob turned. I could see the movement and hear the sound. I quickly hid myself behind the drapery, remembering too late that I had not locked the door after myself.

Peeking out from my hiding place, I saw the door begin to open. My mind worked frantically to manufacture some excuse for my being there and for the presence of the highwayman's spoils. Who could be coming in? Surely not one of the servants. I felt certain that it must be Cousin Bret, who had discovered the booty but who had left it here so that he could use it at his convenience in accusing Mama and forcing Amanda into marrying him.

From the hall I heard a familiar voice say, "I don't believe that's your room, Cummings." I always liked the sound of Sir John's voice, but this time it sounded particularly pleasing to my ear.

"No, it's Robert's room," Cousin Bret admitted. "I thought I would just take a look at it."

"Somehow I doubt that Robert would appreciate your investigating his room," Sir John said in his driest voice.

"I can't think why not."

Despite Cousin Bret's defiance, I could see that he was pulling the door closed, and I heaved a sigh of relief. In a matter of moments I heard both sets of steps leave the area, but I knew that Sir John would manage to keep my cousin away until I had finished my task. In the meantime I tossed the purses, jewels, and loose coins into a sack I had brought for the purpose. All the while I was trying to decide if my original plan would still work.

Thwarted in getting his hands on the stolen goods in Robert's room, Cousin Bret would be searching for their next hiding place, presumably. And his discovery of the strongbox key, as if by accident, would prove too much of a temptation for him to resist. Or so I hoped.

When I had gathered everything from the room, I swung the sack over my shoulder and was surprised at the weight of it. Mama had certainly been an amazingly successful highwayman; you had to give her that! The hallway was clear and I raced along to the back stairs leading up to the attics. Trudging up the narrow steps to the next floor was harder than I'd anticipated, but I was in a hurry now to be finished. I wanted no one else to come upon me before I was finished.

I dumped the bag near the strongbox and allowed myself just a minute in the old rocking chair to catch my breath. When I set to work again I found that all the pieces just barely fit in the strongbox, though it was of a moderate size. I couldn't help but wonder what it was all worth, those rings and purses and pieces of gold. And Mama not the least bit tempted to appropriate them.

After locking the box I went by a circuitous route down through the house and out into the grounds. At the dovecote I felt for the other key and placed this one directly underneath it, so that Amanda could scarcely miss it when she reached in. In her artless fashion she would undoubtedly give away exactly the information that I wanted her to.

Surely Cousin Bret would suspect that Mama had

removed the spoils to the strongbox and hidden the key in the dovecote. I had left the door of Robert's room unlocked so that he could discover that the goods were gone from there. I only hoped his mind would not dwell on the fact that it was Sir John who caught him going into Robert's room. Mightn't Sir John have mentioned the incident to Mama, who would have gotten the wind up? Yes, it could have happened that way, and Cousin Bret had better believe that it had!

At length I returned to my room to dress for dinner. This process had become much more important in the last few weeks. Though we had always dressed to a certain extent, it was nothing like the way we did now, with Sir John there to admire our toilettes. Cousin Bret, unfortunately, made his own share of comments on them, but that was neither here nor there.

Just when I was about to descend, I heard the distant rumbling of thunder and saw a crack of lightning. Well, there would be no walks out in the shrubberies that night, I thought, discouraged. Our scheme for fooling Bret would have to wait and I wasn't just brimming with patience. I wanted the whole mess over and behind us—so that I could concentrate on winning Sir John's love.

·16·

It rained the better part of the next day and we all wandered about the house bumping into one another. Only by early evening were things beginning to clear. Just before dinner I found Amanda in the drawing room before the men and Mama joined us, and I said, "Try to make it tonight. The grass isn't so wet that it will ruin your slippers. And let me know right away when you've shown Cousin Bret the key."

She reluctantly agreed to this, though I could tell that she was concerned about her slippers. When dinner was over and Cousin Bret tried to get her to go walking with him, she fluttered her hands, eyed me rather petulantly, and agreed. Sir John looked amused, but he said nothing. When they had left, Mama urged me to walk out with Sir John. "But you must put a shawl about your shoulders," she insisted. "Run up to your room and get one, so you won't keep Sir John waiting."

I had the distinct impression she wished to have a few words alone with him, but I was unable to linger at the keyhole because the butler was hovering there himself, waiting for a summons to bring in the port or Madeira, which was the usual habit we'd gotten into of an evening.

Instead, I rushed up to my room, grabbed the first shawl that came to hand, though it did not perfectly match my dress, and skipped back downstairs to see if I might make another attempt at listening in on their conversation. But there was silence in the room when I got there, and chagrined, I merely walked in and found them sitting in adjacent chairs, puzzling over an old book of Papa's about the family.

We passed Amanda and Cousin Bret on our way farther out onto the grounds. She gave me a conspiratorial nod, but her brow had that puzzled wrinkle that told me they had also discovered the strongbox key. Very good. Knowing my cousin, he wouldn't let any grass grow beneath his feet. I could count on his claiming the key and the strongbox that very night.

For Sir John's benefit I rubbed my head the way Mama does when she is about to be communicated by one of her ghosts and said, "I have this feeling that something is going to happen tonight. I see gold and jewels."

Sir John grinned at me. "Your sister isn't very adept at playing these games, is she? If Cummings hadn't been looking in the other direction, he would surely have wondered why she winked with such ferocity."

"Don't be too hard on her. She has managed to bring it off just fine, I would say. You can tell Cousin Bret is already scheming to get his hands on the strongbox."

"He *was* rather transparent, wasn't he?" Sir John agreed.

There was something a little unusual about his own actions, it seemed to me. For one thing, he'd made not the slightest effort to kiss me, even when Amanda was out of view. And he held my arm in a rather formal way, not hugging it so warmly against his body as he usually did.

Thinking that he might be offended that I hadn't given him a bigger role in the coming activities, I said, "If you wish, I will allow you to be the one to discover my cousin with the strongbox. He might not take me as seriously as he would take you, in any case.''

We had arrived at the little wooden bridge over the stream. The trees on either side seemed to cast wide shadows. In this secluded spot I felt certain that Sir John would at last take me into his arms. But he did nothing of the sort.

He stood towering over me, staring down into my eyes with his usual expressiveness. ''You've become quite trusting in your attitude toward me. It's certainly a change, and a welcome one. In fact, I have a good mind to run off to the border with you this very night, rather than wait for the Public Day confusion.''

I blinked at him. He was referring to the letter I had sent Robert. ''How could you possibly know? Has he written to you? It was only a joke, you know. Nothing to put you out of countenance.''

''Well, if he kills me in a duel for it, you will have only yourself to blame. Robert would not take kindly to the idea of his sister eloping, even with his best friend.''

I snorted. ''He was not supposed to challenge you to a duel. He was supposed to come down to Cambridgeshire so that he might sort out the whole mess.''

''You gave him very little choice,'' a voice behind us said dryly.

I hadn't heard his voice in such a long time. Stupidly, tears sprang to my eyes. I swung around and threw myself on his chest as he emerged from the shadows. ''You did come, you silly, wonderful fellow. Now everything will be all right.''

''I'm sure I don't know why you thought I couldn't handle it myself,'' Sir John protested, laughing. ''Robert is such a scatterbrain that he's likely to make a muddle of it.''

I paid no heed to his teasing. It was so good to see Robert. I had forgotten how solid and handsome he

was, with his shock of dark-brown hair and steady
green eyes. He stood only a few inches taller than me,
not nearly so tall as Sir John. "Mama will be so happy
that you're here," I sighed. "She's very much in need
of your guidance, so long as it isn't unbearably self-
righteous. She couldn't bear that."

"I understand. I believe you've done very well in
my absence."

Whether this was true or not, I was so pleased to
hear him say it that I almost missed Sir John's next
comments.

"We think it would be best if Robert waited to see
her until the morning. That is, I suspect something is
going to happen tonight that would best be handled by
your brother and myself, with your mother and sister
quite uninvolved."

I wondered if Sir John had told Robert all about
Mama being the highwayman, and I raised an inquiring gaze to his face.

"Yes, he knows. In fact, he knows a great deal,
because you refused to trust me earlier."

Something about the way he said this made me
blush. Surely he hadn't told Robert about our various
interludes. They were, after all, a very private matter.
But I couldn't get him to look me directly in the eye,
and Robert's mind was already on the night ahead.

"What if Cousin Bret simply decides to take off with
the spoils?"

I didn't think that was very likely. "He has made
the most determined effort to get Amanda to marry
him, you see. The jewels and money could not amount
to anything near as much as Hastings and all our family possessions."

"Which he was not likely to intimidate me into giving him, was he?"

"You weren't here," I reminded him.

"My emissary was," he assured me, nodding to Sir John.

Something about the baronet's smugness at this point made me feel saucy. "But Sir John has been a little distracted by certain elements of his visit. Perhaps he has not been thinking as clearly as you might have hoped."

"I'll have you know I have been thinking perfectly clearly," Sir John said as he pulled me close to him and tucked my arm through his. "Little distractions cannot induce me to forget the call of duty."

"Little? Ha."

Robert shook his head with amusement. "We'll discuss that further tomorrow. Right now we have to concentrate on ridding ourselves of Cousin Bret once and for all."

The best view of the dovecote was from Robert's room. Robert had gone straight there as secretly as possible. Sir John and I joined him after we left Cousin Bret for the night. There was only a faint moonlight, but it was easy enough to see my cousin saunter to the dovecote and reach his hand up for the key. He pocketed it as casually as he might have his own handkerchief. What a dastardly fellow he is.

And then he headed directly into the house. He could not even have stopped at his room, he was so quickly near the attic door. From his years of visiting us, he knew where the strongbox was. It didn't even occur to him that it might have been moved because it was now being used as a repository for stolen goods.

Hiding in the dark of Robert's room with the door slightly ajar, we heard Cousin Bret move quickly down the hall toward the entrance to the attics. I peeked around the corner of the corridor and saw that he had a candle shedding a very small amount of light on the area before him.

On tiptoe we moved down the hall toward the door. Above us we could hear the dragging of the old box away from its companions so that Cousin Bret could more easily get at the lock. Robert now motioned me behind him in preparation for the big act we had planned. Sir John waited downstairs in the corridor just in case my cousin should try to break and run.

As though he suspected only a friendly though misguided servant to be at fault for making noise in the middle of the night, Robert called, "Who's up there? This is not the time of day for someone to be working in the attics; you'll wake the entire household."

I could hear Cousin Bret's sharp intake of breath. Not in a million years would he have suspected that Robert might be home or that he would be in a position to discover him at his night's work.

"I was just looking for something up here," he called back, hastily slamming the top down on the strongbox.

Robert made his way quickly up the rest of the stairs and stood like a giant at the top of them, frowning down at my cousin, who was still trying to get the lock attached.

"I had no idea you were home," Cousin Bret squeaked, his fingers working frantically. "Imagine your arriving without my being told! How very strange of your family."

"No one," Robert said, and then added, "except Catherine, knows that I've arrived. It was too late to wake them. What is it you're doing, Cousin Bret?"

"Oh, nothing, nothing. I was just looking for a costume for Public Day. Your family is thinking of having a costume ball, and when I found that I couldn't sleep, I thought I would just take a look up here."

"But why the old strongbox? We've never kept clothing in it."

"No? Well, I didn't know."

"And the key. Where did you come by the key?" Robert's brow had puckered with concern. "It's not really something one of our visitors should have hold of, you know."

"I just happened to come upon it. Actually, I was walking with Amanda when she noticed it in a very strange place."

"Where was that?"

I could scarcely keep from laughing by this point, watching my cousin wriggle and twist to get out of this jam.

"In the old dovecote. Where you apparently kept a key to get into the house when you were out late at night."

"I certainly never had the strongbox key out there." Robert sounded astonishingly disbelieving. "Perhaps you would give me the key, Cousin Bret."

Oh, the reluctance he showed. I thought for a moment that he was going to toss the key somewhere deep in the bowels of the attic where we would have the devil of a time finding it. But no, he slowly handed it to Robert, though he protested the whole while, "I hadn't even a chance to open the box," he insisted. "I had just gotten up here when you came."

"Surely that can't be true," Robert demurred. "I heard the sound of someone dragging a heavy object across the floor. That is what first called my attention to you." He stooped down in front of the box and inserted the key. I felt that my cousin had begun to hold his breath.

With a small scraping sound, Robert turned the key and the lock sprung open. He lifted the lid and simply sat there for a long moment. Inside were all the valuables, the purses, and rings, and gold and silver and all sorts of coins that Mama had collected. Robert whistled. Then he leaned back on his haunches and glared up at Cousin Bret.

"What is this doing here? These are without doubt ill-gotten gains. How did you come by them, cousin?"

"They aren't mine," Cousin Bret protested. "They're your mother's."

Robert laughed. I've never heard him laugh so gleefully and so apparently freely. He laughed so hard that tears came to his eyes, and he seemed almost unable to stop. "My mother's," he finally repeated, before going off into gales of laughter again. "Oh, that's a good one."

I shifted farther back into the shadows. No need for Cousin Bret to notice me at a time like this and demand that I side with him. Robert had the situation well under control.

"But you can't send him off accused of stealing from the neighbors," Mama protested when Robert told her that Cousin Bret had left and would not be returning. "He had nothing to do with it."

"Oh, but he did," Robert assured her. "He had every intention of using his knowledge as a way of forcing Amanda to marry him and getting as much benefit out of Hastings as possible. You needn't think he's an honorable man, my dear Mama. He would use whatever subterfuge he could to get his way. This will give us all the added satisfaction of never having to tolerate him at Hastings again. A very nice reward indeed."

"Well, I must say I didn't expect him to cave in so easily to your demand," I remarked. "We'd have had the devil of a time trying to prove he had anything to do with highway robbery."

"Not such a very difficult time," Robert argued. "There was the stable lad who saw him several times take Thunder out in the middle of the night. And nights when there was a visit from the highwayman, at that."

"We didn't have any intention of trying to prove

it,'' Sir John interposed. ''Just to make sure there were
various other elements working to convince him of the
necessity of departing for his dear home at the soonest
moment. But we could have managed, all of us, to cast
the gravest suspicion on him. As it is, the constable
has by now stumbled over the box of spoils left outside
his door like a foundling.''

Robert nodded. ''He'll manage to return them to
their proper owners.'' He gave Mama a stern look and
she waved nervous fingers at him.

''I shan't do it again, I promise. There will be plenty
of other things to see to, especially with a wedding in
the offing.''

''Whose wedding is in the offing?'' I demanded.

''Yours, for one,'' Sir John informed me. ''I'm sure
you will wish to protest and I'll be glad to hear every
word of it, but not at this particular moment, my love.
Assure yourself that both your mother and your brother
have given me their permission to address you, which
I intend to do at any moment now, if I can pull you
away from this intriguing scene.''

Mama smiled benignly on us and Robert waved a
hand to indicate that we had his full cooperation in our
endeavor to withdraw from the family. So I gave in to
Sir John's insistent tug on my hand and allowed myself
to be drawn away from the two of them. Amanda was
not a party to all of this. It would have been too much
for her nerves—or so she said when Robert tried to
include her.

It soon became clear that Sir John had no intention
of doing things in the proper way. Well, every girl
expects the man to get down on his knees and protest
his undying love, doesn't she? Sir John was satisfied
with circling me in his arms, out in the orchard, and
kissing me most thoroughly. This, I supposed, was all
the pleading I was going to get from him. I protested.

"Don't you think you could at least squat down just the tiniest bit?" I asked.

"Whatever for?"

"Well, I thought that was how it was done, Sir John. I thought the gentleman was supposed to indicate that he would be putting his lady on a pedestal, you know."

"Rest assured I would never do anything of the sort. And, Catherine, I think it is high time you learned to call me John. There's a formality about Sir John that doesn't sit well with me when I think of holding you in my arms."

"Hmmm. Already he is making demands on me. I wonder where it will end."

"Oh, I'm sure you have a good idea of where it will end. And I don't think you're altogether worried about that."

I smiled beatifically. "No, not about that. But, John, what of the other commands you are likely to impose on me? Look what that sort of thing did to my mother. She was so unstrung by the lack of commands and guidance after my father died that she went a little dotty."

"I don't think that's something we're going to have to worry about. For one thing, I'm not the same kind of man your father was, am I? He was very proper and strict, and I assure you I'm not the least bit that way, myself. And as for you, wild as the streak that runs through you is, there's a sensible woman who inhabits that body, too, and one who doesn't need any outside strictures to make her behave in a reasonably acceptable way."

"Ha!" I snorted. "Little do you know."

"I know enough. You're not the same woman your mother is, sweetings."

"Sweetings! How positively mushy. Is that what you consider romantic?"

"No, it's just something I've wanted a chance to call

you. So, Catherine, what is your answer to my proposal? Will you have me?''

I cocked my head at him, trying hard to delay my response so that he would have to worry for a few minutes. ''It seems to me that you have some explaining to do first. Why did you try to make up to Amanda when you came?''

Oh, I shan't ever forget the wicked sparkle that appeared in his eyes then. ''Couldn't you guess? Catherine, seeing you in the pond and sparring verbally with you very nearly set me on my ear. But I absolutely refused to accept that I'd been struck a blow from which I had no chance of recovering. Instead, I threw up as much obstruction and denial as I could. You know perfectly well that Amanda never held the least interest for me. It was all a ruse to keep myself from recognizing that I had fallen madly in love with you.''

Now this was the kind of romantic talk I'd wanted to hear. My efforts to prolong it, however, were all in vain. I was so in love with him that I pressed my cheek against his and whispered in his ear, ''Yes, I'll have you, you dreadful man. How could I be satisfied with less now that I've found you?''

He pulled me closer to him and whispered back, ''I love you to distraction, you irrepressible woman. What a marriage we shall have! Can you picture how it will be? Wild and free and quite the most comfortable union you can imagine, because we are like to like, and yet we're not in just the ordinary mold. Do you suppose people will think us eccentric one of these days?''

''Certainly by the time we're grown old,'' I replied. ''Oh, John, what a time we'll have. I can hardly wait to be off with you. Do you think we will have to wait and see if Mama is to be trusted with her new resolve?''

''I haven't the slightest doubt that she can be trusted, with Robert's capable guidance. He'll not be too restricting. And your mother will be too busy getting ready for our wedding and planning for Amanda's Season to need any other distraction. Besides, her Cavalier ghost has abandoned her, thank heaven. We can post the banns now and be married within a fortnight. My mother won't mind the rush, since it will mean someone has finally managed to settle me down.''

"I promise not to tell her that I haven't,'' I said happily as I leaned against his strong frame. His arms went instantly around me and my heartbeat quickened. I waited, as always, for the wondrous touch of his lips . . .

And that is how it all happened, more or less. Except for the tale of how Robert and John managed to spike the earl's guns the next time he sent a letter to the newspaper. I don't consider that nearly as interesting as the rest of the story. *He* says I might as well have included it. But I shan't.

If I am ever moved to take pen in hand again, I shall probably make Amanda my heroine, for though she is not so lively as a heroine ought to be, still her adventures in London with Mama as her chaperone do have a touch of the extraordinary about them. I would have to give her an assumed name, however, for if I am going to write a second history, I most assuredly intend to offer it for publication. Once as a labor of love is one thing; a second would be far too much effort not to be shared with an audience larger than one.

Speaking of John, my only audience, he and I were quite right about our love and our happiness. He is even rather pleased, now that I have finished it, to read of himself as the hero of my tale.

And if the world considers us an eccentric pair, so much the better!